Please return this book on or before the date shown above. To renew go to www.essex.gov.uk/libraries, ring 0845 603 7628 or go to any Essex library.

Dear Reader

Sometimes you really, really fall in love with a hero. And I fell head over heels for Rhys. Firstly, he's a fabulous doctor—caring, gentle, and very good at what he does. Secondly, he has the most gorgeous voice. And thirdly, he understands Katrina's hearing problem—he rescues her when she needs it, just as my husband rescues me when I haven't caught what someone has said.

I also fell for Katrina's family—because they remind me of mine! The kind of people who'll celebrate the good times with you and always be there for you in the bad: the kind of family my hero Rhys has never had, but definitely deserves.

As I was writing the wedding scene, I was privileged to attend a special family wedding (my daughter was the flower girl). It was in a beautiful little country church, and I couldn't resist borrowing both the wedding cake and the weather from the day! That's why I've dedicated this book to my cousin Lee and his lovely bride Lucy, with congratulations and lots of love.

I'm always delighted to hear from readers, so do come and visit me at www.katehardy.com

With love

Kate Hardy

Kate Hardy lives in Norwich, in the east of England, with her husband, two young children, one bouncy spaniel, and too many books to count! When she's not busy writing romance or researching local history, she helps out at her children's schools. She also loves cooking—spot the recipes sneaked into her books! (They're also on her website, along with extracts and stories behind the books.) Writing for Mills & Boon has been a dream come true for Kate—something she wanted to do ever since she was twelve. She's been writing Medical™ Romances for nearly seven years now, and also writes for Modern Heat™. She says it's the best of both worlds, because she gets to learn lots of new things when she's researching the background to a book: add a touch of passion, drama and danger, a new gorgeous hero every time, and it's the perfect job!

Kate's always delighted to hear from readers, so do drop in to her website at www.katehardy.com

Recent titles by the same author:

Medical™ Romance
THE SPANISH DOCTOR'S LOVE-CHILD
THE DOCTOR'S ROYAL LOVE-CHILD
  (Brides of Penhally Bay)
THE ITALIAN GP'S BRIDE

Modern Heat™
HOTLY BEDDED, CONVENIENTLY WEDDED
SOLD TO THE HIGHEST BIDDER!
BREAKFAST AT GIOVANNI'S

THE CHILDREN'S DOCTOR'S SPECIAL PROPOSAL

BY
KATE HARDY

All the characters in this book have no existence outside
the imagination of the author, and have no relation
whatsoever to anyone bearing the same name or names.
They are not even distantly inspired by any individual
known or unknown to the author, and all the incidents
are pure invention.

First published in Great Britain 2009
Large Print edition 2009
Harlequin Mills & Boon Limited,
Eton House, 18-24 Paradise Road,
Richmond, Surrey TW9 1SR

© Pamela Brooks 2009

ISBN: 978 0 263 20531 2

Set in Times Roman 16½ on 19 pt.
17-0909-50494

Harlequin Mills & Boon policy is to use papers that are
natural, renewable and recyclable products and made
from wood grown in sustainable forests. The logging and
manufacturing process conform to the legal environmental
regulations of the country of origin.

Printed and bound in Great Britain
by CPI Antony Rowe, Chippenham, Wiltshire

What people are saying about Kate Hardy…

'THE ITALIAN GP'S BRIDE is a
spellbinding romance that I devoured
in a single sitting! Kate Hardy is a
fabulously talented writer whose books
never fail to make me laugh, cry and care, and
THE ITALIAN GP'S BRIDE is the latest in a
long line of captivating romances that have
made her one of my all-time favourite writers.'
–*Cataromance on THE ITALIAN GP'S BRIDE,
Medical*™ *Romance August 07*

Look out for Kate Hardy in Modern Heat™**!**

'BREAKFAST AT GIOVANNI'S is simply
terrific! Sexy, funny, tender, passionate and
romantic, this engrossing tale features a loveable
heroine and a gorgeous Italian hero who will make
you swoon! Kate Hardy is a writer readers can
count on in order to deliver an entertaining page-
turner which they will devour in a single sitting,
and BREAKFAST AT GIOVANNI'S is certainly
no exception. So take the phone off the hook,
put your feet up and lose yourself…'
—*Cataromance on BREAKFAST AT GIOVANNI'S,
July 07*

Kate Hardy is an award-winning author.

For Lee and Lucy,
with love

CHAPTER ONE

'WELCOME back.' Lynne greeted Katrina with a broad smile. 'So how was Italy?'

'Fabulous. Italy in late September is just perfect. It's my new favourite place in the world,' Katrina said. 'Pompeii was stunning. And the Blue Grotto. And…' She laughed. 'That isn't what you really want to know, is it? Yes, I brought Italian biscuits back for the ward. Seriously nice ones.' She dangled a carrier bag in front of the charge nurse. 'A big tin of them.'

'Good girl.' Lynne patted her on the back. 'Just what we all wanted to hear. Though I'm glad you had a good time on holiday.'

'How's Sadie doing?' Katrina asked, walking with Lynne to the kitchen and placing the biscuit tin on the worktop along with a note saying, *Help yourself, with love from Kat.*

'Fine. Though she's been missing your

stories and wants to know when Doc-a-rina's coming back.'

'Oh, bless.' Sadie, a two-year-old with a clicky hip that had been reset by the orthopaedic surgeon, was one of Katrina's favourites; even though lying on a cot in traction must have been uncomfortable for the little girl, she never once complained and always had a huge smile for the medical staff. 'I'll go and see her in a minute before I start the ward rounds.' Katrina switched on the kettle, then she slapped a hand to her forehead. 'I almost forgot. The new consultant.' He'd started the day after she'd gone on holiday, and she'd been off duty the day he'd come for his interview and a look round the ward, so she hadn't yet met him. 'What's he like?'

Lynne nodded with obvious approval. 'Gorgeous. And as soon as you hear that voice you just want it to start whispering sweet nothings to you.'

'Except he's unavailable because, like you, he was snapped up as a teenager?' Katrina teased.

'Nobody has a clue, but I'd say probably not. He's excellent with the children, he's polite and pleasant to the parents and the staff, but as for what makes him tick…' Lynne shook her head ruefully. 'Your guess is as good as mine. He's refused every single invite to a team night out so far—politely, but very definitely.'

Katrina frowned. Most new consultants would accept every invitation going in the first couple of weeks, to help them get to know the team outside work and bond with them. 'He's not one of those who spend the bare minimum of time here and as much as possible in private practice, is he?' she asked.

Lynne shook her head. 'Far from it. He puts in the hours. He stays late—and if he does leave early, he'll either ring in or come back to chase up some results.'

A workaholic, then, Katrina thought. Just as long as he didn't expect everyone else to follow his lead—it wouldn't be fair on colleagues who happened to have young families. 'What's he like to work with?' she asked.

'Quick, intuitive and—well, you're about to find out for yourself. He's just walked in.' Lynne glanced towards the door. 'Morning, Dr Morgan.'

'Rhys,' the doctor corrected with a smile.

And what a smile.

Lynne was right, Katrina thought. Rhys Morgan was absolutely gorgeous. Tall, with dark hair and fair skin and blue, blue eyes—pure Celtic colouring. And with a name like Rhys Morgan, she would've been very surprised had his voice not had that faint Welsh lilt.

That incredibly *sexy* Welsh lilt.

And an incredibly sensual mouth.

She pushed the thought away. Rhys Morgan was her new colleague, and she didn't date colleagues. Not since Pete. She didn't make the same mistake twice.

'Good morning, Lynne,' he said.

'Rhys, this is Katrina Gregory, our senior house officer.' Lynne introduced them swiftly. 'Kat, this is Rhys Morgan, our new consultant.'

'Hello, Rhys. Good to meet you,' Katrina said, and stretched out her hand.

When he took it, she was surprised by the jolt of awareness that shot through her. One that was clearly mutual and just as surprising for him, judging by the way his eyes widened very slightly. But then he seemed to regain his control and gave her a polite smile, releasing her hand. 'Hello, Katrina.'

'The kettle's about to boil and our rounds don't start for another ten minutes. Coffee?' Katrina asked.

'Thanks. Black, no sugar, please.'

She spooned instant coffee into three mugs, adding sugar to Lynne's and milk to her own before pouring on boiling water and handing the first mug to Rhys. 'Help yourself to biscuits while you still get a chance. As soon as Lynne spreads the word, they'll be gone.' She glanced at her watch. 'And if you'll excuse me, I want to pop in and see Sadie before we start, to let her know I'm back.'

'Sadie? The little girl with the clicky hip?' he asked.

Katrina nodded. 'Lynne tells me she's been missing my stories.'

He looked slightly disapproving. 'As a doctor, you need to keep a certain amount of distance. Don't get too emotionally involved with your patients.'

'I hardly think telling a story to a little girl who's bed-bound is getting emotionally involved.' And just who did Rhys Morgan think he was, telling her what to do? He may be the new consultant and, strictly speaking, her senior, but that didn't mean he could tell her how to do her job. In her experience, taking a little extra time with their patients often did wonders—it helped them to settle, and she believed that anything that made the hospital a less scary experience for them was a good thing. 'I enjoy my job, and I'm not going to apologise for taking five minutes of my own time to make a child's day that little bit brighter. Excuse me,' she said coolly. 'I'll be back in time for ward rounds.'

When Katrina walked into the cubicle, Sadie's delighted smile took away that rattled feeling she'd had since meeting Rhys Morgan. 'Doc-a-rina!'

'Miss me, poppet?' Katrina sat on the chair beside her, and ruffled her hair. 'What a lovely welcome-back smile.'

'Story?' Sadie begged.

'Later today. After you've had your lunch and I'm on my break,' Katrina promised. 'Hello, Jo,' she said, turning to Sadie's mother. 'I'll be doing the ward rounds in a few minutes, but I wanted to pop in and see you first. How's it going?'

'Dr Morgan says she's doing really well. Hopefully we can go home at the end of the week—not that it's horrible here,' Jo hastened to add.

'But there's no place like home,' Katrina finished, understanding just what Jo meant.

'Good holiday?' Jo asked.

'Brilliant, thanks. I must be three inches shorter after all that walking, but it was worth it.'

Jo laughed. 'If I'd known you wanted to be three inches shorter…'

'Sorry. My cousin Maddie has first dibs on my spare height,' Katrina teased back. 'I'll see you later. And my story for you today, Miss Sadie,' she added, smiling at the little girl, 'is all about a princess. Because when I was away I actually saw a magic cave—the one where a princess met the prince from under the sea.'

'Mermaid,' Sadie said happily.

'Something like that,' Katrina said. 'See you soon.'

When Katrina joined Rhys for the ward rounds, she discovered that he was exactly as Lynne had described. Pleasant to the children, polite to their parents and patient enough to answer every single question and explain in more detail when it was needed. Professionally, she couldn't fault him.

And yet there was a reserve about him. Some kind of invisible wall. Like Lynne, Katrina couldn't quite work out what made him tick.

She put it out of her mind so she could concentrate on her patients in the children's assessment clinic for the rest of the morning, and then caught up with her cousin over lunch.

'Welcome home, hon.' Madison hugged her. 'You look fabulous. Though I still think you were mad, going on a walking tour of the Amalfi coast.'

'I saw a lot more than I would've done if I'd been stuck on a beach,' Katrina pointed out.

'So did you meet a gorgeous Italian prince while you were away?'

Madison really was incorrigible, Katrina thought. 'No, but I'm making up a story for Sadie. About the prince from under the sea.' She laughed. 'Right up your street. Or it would have been, had you not met Theo.' She paused. Madison had her finger on the pulse. She might know more about Rhys Morgan. 'Have you met our new consultant yet?' she asked, trying her best to sound casual.

'Rhys Morgan?' Madison nodded. 'I called him into Theatre last week during a difficult birth—and the baby was absolutely fine, before you ask. He's a nice guy. Knows his stuff but doesn't throw his weight around.'

Oh, doesn't he? Katrina thought, remembering what he'd said about Sadie.

Madison's eyes sparkled. 'Since you're asking about him, Kat, does that mean you're—?'

'No, it doesn't,' Katrina interrupted, guessing what her cousin was about to ask. Since she'd found happiness with Theo, Madison had been trying to find the same for her cousin, and the matchmaking was driving Katrina crazy. 'He's nice enough, as you say—a good doctor—but he's a bit reserved. And he told me off this morning for getting too emotionally involved with my patients.'

'He has a point, hon. You *do* get too close to your patients,' Madison said gently.

Katrina rolled her eyes. 'I love my job. I love the ward. And, actually, telling stories to the kids is good for *me*. It's the best stress-reliever I know, going off into a world of make-believe and seeing all these little faces smiling back at me.'

'But you still worry about them when you get home. You never quite switch off.'

'It goes with the territory.' Katrina glanced at her watch. 'I'd better get back. I promised Sadie a story over lunch, and I don't want to upset the new consultant by being late for ward rounds this afternoon.'

'Sounds to me as if you just got off on the wrong foot with each other. Give the guy a chance. He's OK.' Madison paused, looking concerned. 'Not all men are like Pete, you know.'

'I know that.' Katrina rolled her eyes. 'But not all men are potential partners, either. I'm happy to keep men as friends and colleagues.'

'Hmm. When you find the right one, you'll change your mind.'

Katrina ruffled her cousin's hair. 'I know you've found Mr Right, but it doesn't happen for everyone. Anyway, I like my life as it is. I love my job, I have good friends, and I have the best family in the world. Not to mention the fact I'm going to be an auntie and godmother to the most gorgeous little girl in about four months' time.' Madison's amniocentesis results had come through just before Katrina had left for Italy; to everyone's huge relief, all was well. 'I don't need anyone, Maddie. I'm happy as I am.'

'If you say so,' Madison said.

'I do.' And the fact that she couldn't get Rhys Morgan's incredibly blue eyes out of her head, the fact that they reminded her of the colour of the sea on the Amalfi coast—well, that was just post-holiday silliness, Katrina told herself sternly. 'I'll see you later.'

She had enough time to tell Sadie a story about the princess and the merman meeting in the magic grotto, and then it was time to face Rhys again.

'I see you admitted a couple of patients from the assessment clinic this morning,' Rhys said.

He'd been in a different clinic that morning—so when had he had time to check what she'd been doing? Or maybe he'd just caught sight of the ward's whiteboard where they listed the patients and their named nurses and he wanted a quick rundown on what she'd done before they did the ward round. Fair enough. She didn't have any doubts about her clinical judgement.

'There's Jennie Myerson—the GP sent her in because her face was swollen, her blood pressure and temperature were up, she said her joints hurt, and there was blood in her urine,' she explained.

'She's not on medication for anything, so it's not an allergic reaction, but apparently she did have a sore throat a couple of weeks ago. So I wonder if it's a staph infection causing interstitial nephritis.'

'You've given her something for the blood pressure and paracetamol to deal with the pain and get her temperature down,' he said, reading swiftly through the notes.

'I also took bloods and I asked if her urine output could be measured. Are the results back from the lab yet?'

'Not according to these notes.'

'Then I'll chase them after the ward round. But if I'm right and her ESR and urea are up, I'd like to do a renal ultrasound.'

'I think you're going to be right,' he said, surprising her. 'Her urine output's way below what it should be. Did you ask if she's allergic to penicillin?'

'Yes, and there's no family history, so they don't think so.'

'Good. You talk to the lab while I sort the ultrasound on her kidney. If the blood results are what you think they'll be, we'll start her on penicillin. This sort of condition can make a little one feel really rough.'

He went through the other patients on their list equally thoroughly, taking account of what Katrina said and also of the observations recorded by the nurses. Definitely a team player, Katrina thought. Someone who listened to others. Which was a good thing, as far as the ward was concerned.

So why was there still that wall between them?

Because, although Rhys was great to work with—intuitive, quick to sum up what was going on, understanding how their patients felt and calming the parents' worries as they went from bed to bed—she was aware of a definite barrier between them. He barely even made eye contact with her.

Had it not been for Lynne's comment earlier, she would've thought maybe it was just her. Although he hadn't seemed to have a problem with her clinical judgement, he'd made it clear earlier that he thought she was too emotionally involved with their patients.

And there had been that weird prickle of awareness when he'd shaken her hand, which she was pretty sure he'd felt, too. Maybe this distance was his way of telling her that he had no intention of acting on it.

Well, that was fine by her. Because she didn't want to act on it, either. She'd learned her lesson well: getting involved with a colleague was the quickest way to heartache. Never, ever again.

Later that afternoon, Rhys was walking past the ward's playroom to his office when he heard laughter. Loud laughter. As if the children in the playroom were watching some kind of show, rather than being the general hum of noise of little ones playing independently. He couldn't remember anyone talking about a visitor coming to entertain the children, and he knew there wasn't a television in the playroom. So what was going on? Curious, he looked through the doorway.

And there at the far end of the room was Katrina. Sitting on a beanbag, with her feet tucked under her, surrounded by the more mobile children from the ward and what looked like most of the children from the waiting room. At first he thought she was reading them a story—and then he realised that she wasn't holding a book. The story she was telling was straight out of her head, illustrated by a couple of glove puppets. She was getting the children involved, too—asking them questions so they made suggestions to shape the story, and persuading them all to join in with a simple song or a chorus.

He glanced at his watch. She should have been off duty half an hour ago. Yet here she was, entertaining the children.

This went beyond dedication.

Katrina Gregory clearly loved her job.

And the children clearly loved her all the way back. He'd noticed on the ward rounds how the newer parents turned straight to her for comfort, how the older ones greeted her as a friend. How the children brightened when they saw her and even the sickest ones could summon up a smile for Dr Katrina. Her warmth suffused everyone.

Even himself.

And, lord, he was tempted. Katrina was gorgeous. And it wasn't just her personality: her midnight-blue eyes were stunning and her mouth was lush enough to make any man sit up and beg.

When she'd shaken hands with him that morning, he'd been incredibly aware of her—of the softness of her skin, the light floral scent she wore, the quiet yet clear voice.

Irresistible.

He'd wanted her immediately.

And had held himself back, because it was highly unlikely a woman that attractive would still be single. Even though she didn't wear a ring at work—he'd actually caught himself checking, during the ward round—she probably kept it on a chain round her neck, tucked inside her shirt for safety and staying close to her heart. And even if he'd got it wrong and Katrina was free, he was hardly in a position to offer her anything. His last girlfriend had told him he was so distant he might as well have been in Australia when they'd gone out together—and he knew she'd had a point. He was lousy at relationships, so it was best to stick to what he was good at. Work.

Katrina Gregory was his colleague—full stop and end of story.

Quietly, Rhys left the doorway and headed for his office.

CHAPTER TWO

THE following morning, Katrina was on her way out of Sadie's cubicle when she saw Rhys in the corridor. 'Morning,' she said brightly, hoping that he wasn't going to give her another lecture about being too close to her patients but quite ready to battle her corner if she had to.

'Morning.' He gave her one of the slow, sweet smiles he'd given Lynne in the kitchen the previous day—the smile that had made Katrina's knees go ever so slightly weak—and all her annoyance melted away. 'I'm with you in the children's assessment clinic this morning.'

'I thought I was on with Tim,' she said. Their first-year foundation doctor was working mainly with her in the assessment clinic and she was enjoying his enthusiasm and freshness.

'He called in sick this morning—he's caught

the tummy bug that's going round. So I'm afraid you're stuck with me,' he said lightly.

'I think I can manage,' she said, equally lightly. Funny how the look in his eyes was making her heart beat that little bit faster. She really needed to get a grip. 'Not that I'm trying to patronise you, but have you worked in the assessment clinic here before? I mean, you know how the system works?'

'It'll be my first time,' Rhys said, 'but I gather our patients are referred by their GPs or by the emergency department staff.'

She nodded. 'We have a couple of paediatric nurses who do the usual checks when the children are brought in—height, weight, temperature, pulse, breathing rate, urine sample—and take a medical history, then we see the children in the order in which they arrive. Unless there's an emergency, of course,' she added, 'but we do warn parents that emergencies take priority.'

'Sounds like the same set-up we had back at the Cardiff Memorial Hospital,' he said. 'That's fine by me. Do you want a coffee before we start?'

She glanced at her watch. 'We haven't really got time—not unless we make it with half-cold water. Who's doing ward rounds this morning, if you're not?'

'Will.'

Will was the senior consultant: a tall, jolly man who had a fund of terrible jokes and even more terrible ties that their patients all loved. She grinned. 'The poor nurses—not to mention the patients—will need sunglasses! At least your taste in ties is bearable.'

'I wouldn't bet on that.' His eyes glittered with mischief. 'This is my third week here. I think it's time to start a competition with Will in neckwear.'

She groaned. 'Don't tell me your wife and kids find them for you, too.'

'Not married. No kids. No intention of having either.'

His voice was suddenly cool, breaking the light-hearted mood, and Katrina winced inwardly. Hadn't Lynne said yesterday that the man was very guarded about his private life? 'Sorry. I wasn't fishing. Just that Will always says his wife and kids buy his loudest ties, and I assumed if you had a collection like his it'd be from the same kind of source.' She raked a hand through her hair. 'Look, I didn't mean to pry. I apologise.'

'No offence taken.'

But that invisible barrier was back between them again. And this time it felt a tiny bit wider.

Katrina tried her best to keep it professional in the assessment unit, though she was very much aware of Rhys's presence—far more than she usually was with Tim or whoever else worked with her. Even when her back was to the room, she knew the precise moment that Rhys left his cubicle and went to call his next patient. And that was worrying. Why was she so aware of the man?

Her third patient that morning worried her even more. Petros was six, and looked very poorly.

'He's been a bit off-colour for the last two days, tired and feeling sick,' his mother said. 'And his back hurts.'

'His temperature's up and he's a bit short of breath,' Katrina observed.

Mrs Smith nodded. 'And his wee's very dark, even though I've tried to get him to drink plenty of water.'

The little boy had olive skin but there was a definite pallor around his mouth, and the whites of his eyes were slightly yellowish. 'Hello, Petros. I'm Dr Katrina,' she said softly. 'Would you mind if I had a little look at you, please?'

He shrugged listlessly.

'He's really not himself,' Mrs Smith said, biting her lip. 'He's always on the go. He's never this quiet and still.'

Katrina squeezed Mrs Smith's hand. 'Try not to worry,' she said gently. 'He's in the right place. Has anyone else in the family or any of his friends had similar symptoms?'

'Everyone's fine.'

So it was unlikely to be a virus, then. The most likely culprit was a urine infection, but the paediatric nurse had already done a dipstick test and it was clear. She didn't like his breathing rate or temperature, though. 'I'm going to listen to your heart and your breathing now, Petros. And afterwards, if you like, you can listen to Mummy's.'

Petros shook his head but didn't say a word.

'OK. I'll be as quick as I can,' she said, and listened through the stethoscope. 'Big breath in? And out. And in. And out. That's lovely. Well done, sweetheart.' His heart, at least, sounded fine. She was still thinking infection, though. 'Can you open your mouth for me and say "ahh"?' she asked.

Petros did so—the quietest 'ahh' Katrina had heard from a child in a while. There was no sign of infection in his throat, but his mouth and tongue definitely looked pale. 'I'm going to need to take a blood test,' she said to Mrs Smith. 'I think he might be slightly jaundiced, because his eyes are a little bit yellow, so I want to check for that and anaemia.'

'He had jaundice when he was born,' Mrs Smith said. 'But the midwife said it was really common with babies.'

'It is—usually, if they get a bit of sunlight, the jaundice goes away within the first week,' Katrina said.

'It did.'

There was something nagging in the back of Katrina's mind, but she couldn't quite place it. 'It's been a lovely sunny few days, hasn't it?' she asked. 'Have you been doing anything special, Petros?'

'I went to Granddad's garden,' Petros said. 'He grows magic beans.'

'Like *Jack and the Beanstalk*? Wow. Did you meet the giant?' Katrina asked.

The little boy didn't even crack a smile, merely rubbed at his back.

'OK, sweetheart. I'm going to give you something to take that pain away,' she said gently, and gave him two spoonfuls of children's paracetamol syrup. 'This will help you to stop feeling quite so hot, too. Do you like your granddad's garden?'

Petros nodded.

'My father-in-law got an allotment this summer,' Mrs Smith explained. 'He's been growing vegetables and Petros has been helping him. We call the broad beans "magic beans"— you know what it's like, trying to get little ones this age to eat vegetables.'

'Don't I just.' Katrina had played the 'magic' card herself before now with a variety of vegetables and a variety of patients.

'Can I interfere?' Rhys said, coming over to Katrina's workspace.

Well, he was her senior. He had several years' more experience than she did. And if he had any bright ideas, she was willing to listen: in Katrina's view, the patient took priority. 'Be my guest.'

He introduced himself swiftly. 'Mrs Smith, these broad beans you mentioned—has your little boy eaten them before?'

'No. Do you think he might be allergic to them?'

'Not allergic, exactly. Petros is a Greek name, yes?'

She nodded. 'It's my grandfather's name.'

He smiled at her. 'May I ask, which part of Greece does your family come from?'

'My husband's from the East End—well, with a name like Smith that's pretty obvious,' she said wryly, 'but my family's originally from Cyprus. My grandparents came over to London just after the war and started a restaurant.'

'Katrina, when you do that blood sample, can you get it tested for G6PD as well?' Rhys asked.

'Of course.' The pieces clicked into place. 'You think it's favism?'

'Yes—I've seen a few cases in Wales,' he said.

'What's favism?' Mrs Smith asked. 'And what's G6PD?'

'G6PD is a chemical in your body—it stands for glucose 6 phosphate dehydrogenase, but it's a bit of a mouthful so it's known as G6PD for short,' Rhys explained. 'Some people have less than normal amounts in their red blood cells, and it's quite common in people who have a Mediterranean origin. If you don't have enough G6PD, then if you get a fever or take certain medicines or eat broad beans—what they call fava beans in America, which is why it's called "favism"—then the body can't protect your red cells properly and you become anaemic.'

'With this condition, you might also get jaundice—and the symptoms mean you get backache and your urine looks the same colour as tea before you add the milk,' Katrina added.

Mrs Smith nodded in understanding. 'Like Petros's does right now.'

'Obviously we need to check the results of the blood tests,' Katrina said, 'but I think Rhys is right.'

'So can you give him this G-whatever stuff in tablets or something?' Mrs Smith asked.

'I'm afraid there aren't any supplements,' Rhys said. 'We'll check how much iron is in his blood, and if there isn't enough he might need a transfusion—but the good news is that Petros will feel a lot better with some rest and a little bit of oxygen to help him breathe more easily.'

'The condition's not going to affect him day to

day,' Katrina explained, 'but he'll need to avoid certain medications—aspirin, some antibiotics and some antimalarial drugs. I can give you a leaflet explaining all that so you know what to avoid.'

'You'll need to tell your GP as well so it's on his medical record and he isn't given any of the medications he needs to avoid by mistake,' Rhys added. 'And we should warn you now that if he gets an infection in future, it might mean his red cells are affected and he'll get anaemia and jaundice again.'

'And *definitely* no more broad beans,' Katrina said.

'Best to avoid Chinese herbal medicines, too,' Rhys continued. 'And, would you believe, moth-balls? They contain a chemical in that can affect people with G6PD deficiency.'

Mrs Smith looked anxious. 'But he's going to be all right?'

'He's going to be absolutely fine,' Katrina re-assured her, ruffling Petros's hair.

'You said earlier it's common in people from the Mediterranean—so I might have it too?' Mrs Smith asked Rhys.

'No, it's more likely that you're a carrier—the

condition is linked with the X chromosome, so
women tend to be carriers but because men only
have one X chromosome they end up develop-
ing the disease,' he explained.

Mrs Smith bit her lip. 'So it's my fault my
son's ill.'

'Absolutely *not*,' Rhys said emphatically. 'It's
a medical condition and you had no reason to
suspect there was a problem. Whatever you do,
don't blame yourself.'

'And, anyway, you were the one who took him
to the doctor—you did exactly the right thing,'
Katrina added. 'Now, Petros, I need to take a
little tiny sample of your blood so I can test it—
but I have magic cream that means it won't hurt
at all. Is that OK?'

The little boy looked up at his mother and then,
at her encouraging smile, nodded.

'Wonderful. Now, you have to say a magic
word as I put the cream on. Do you know a
magic word?'

'Please,' Petros said.

'Oh, honey. That's lovely.' Katrina's heart
melted. 'And do you know another one that a
magician might say?'

'Abracadabra?' the little boy suggested.

'That's perfect. Now, let's say it together. After three. One, two, three…' She took the pot of local anaesthetic gel. 'Abracadabra.' She applied it to his inner elbow. 'Now, it takes a little while to work, so I'm going to let your mummy tell you a story while I see someone else who's feeling a bit poorly, and then I'll come back and see you, OK?'

The little boy nodded.

'You might see a bit of redness on his skin,' Rhys said to Mrs Smith, 'but that's nothing to worry about—it's part of the way the anaesthetic works.'

'Thank you both so much.' Much of the strain had gone from Mrs Smith's face.

'That's what we're here for,' Rhys said with a smile.

Mrs Smith took Petros back over to the waiting area. After Katrina had seen her next patient, she called Petros back and took the blood sample, chatting to him and telling him some of the awful jokes she'd learned from Will to keep him distracted while she slid the needle into his vein. 'All done. That's brilliant,' she told the little boy, pressing a piece of cotton wool over the site and holding it there for a few seconds before taping it on. 'Did it hurt?'

He shook his head.

'Good.' She turned to Mrs Smith. 'The results should be back later this afternoon—then I'll know a lot more and we can talk it through. I'll come and find you as soon as they're back. I know it's a pain having to wait around, and I'm sorry we can't speed the procedure up at all. But there's a coffee bar just outside the department if you want to go and get a drink, and across the corridor there's a play area—there are loads of books and toys and what have you there.' She smiled at Petros. 'So we'll see you a bit later on, OK, sweetheart?'

He nodded.

'And then I'll be able to make you feel a lot better,' she said.

After the clinic had finished, Rhys looked round for Katrina. She wasn't there, but when he stepped into the corridor he saw her near the double doors. 'Katrina,' he called, 'are you heading for the canteen?'

She ignored him completely, letting the doors swing shut behind her.

Rhys stopped in his tracks, staring after her. She'd just blanked him. Had he upset her by butting in on her patient that morning? She hadn't seemed upset at the time…but maybe she'd put on a professional front for the patient's sake. Fine. He'd have a word with her later, explain that he hadn't intended to cast any aspersions on her ability. From what he'd seen, Katrina was good at her job, and the last thing everyone needed was a personality clash to disrupt the harmony of the ward.

Rather than going to the canteen, he went to the 'grab and go' bar for a coffee and a sandwich that he ate at his desk while sorting out some paperwork.

Mid-afternoon, the same thing happened: he saw Katrina about to enter the staff room, called her name—and she completely ignored him.

Oh, great.

Was she still sore about that morning? Or maybe from the previous day, when he'd reminded her about the importance of professional detachment?

He couldn't let this go on. He didn't want to tackle her about it in the staffroom, though. It would be too public and embarrassing for both of them. No: after their shift, he'd have a quiet word with her in his office and hopefully he'd be able to reach some kind of truce with her.

Lynne called him to examine a patient; on his return, he saw Katrina sitting on the bed next to one of their patients, talking to the parents. Both parents had red eyes, and the child was white-faced. He frowned. Ruby Jeffers had been admitted with meningitis the previous week. He knew she'd been having some hearing problems and she'd had an appointment in the audiology department earlier that day in case the virus had caused damage to the cochlea or inflammation of the auditory nerve. Clearly the news wasn't good, and he wasn't that surprised because he knew that meningitis caused deafness in around seven per cent of children who'd had it.

But what did surprise him was when Katrina pushed her hair up on her left side. What was she doing, showing the little girl a pretty earring or something? Or maybe doing some kind of distracting magic trick, because she pulled something from her ear.

But the little girl still wasn't smiling.

He frowned, drawing closer, and heard a snatch of conversation. 'See? It's really easy to take out. And easy to put in. It doesn't hurt because it's made to measure.'

What was?

'What they do, they have some special stuff to make a mould. It looks like play dough and it's pink and purple. They mix it together—and then they put it into your ear. It feels a bit weird, but it doesn't hurt. You can feel it getting a little bit warmer, and then when they take it out they've got the exact shape of your ear and they can make you a special mould that fits your ear only.'

Ear? Mould?

Everything suddenly fell into place.

Ruby's audiology test must have shown that she had hearing loss—if a further test in six weeks didn't show a marked improvement it was very likely that she would need a hearing aid. But the way Katrina was talking felt personal— as if she knew exactly what it felt like, rather than what the audiology team had told her.

'And you know that test you did, where you had to listen for the beeps? That showed the audiologist what you could hear. So then they can programme the hearing aid to help you hear the bits you can't hear right now, but they don't make the bits that you *can* hear any louder.'

'And it doesn't hurt?' Ruby asked.

'Nope. Once it's in, I forget it's even there—like I said, it's made to fit you perfectly, and only you. Feel. It's not heavy, is it?'

Rhys realised then that Katrina was definitely talking personally.

She wore a hearing aid.

'And watch this.' Katrina lifted her hair again, took the aid from the little girl's hand and slipped it back into her ear. 'Push this switch to turn it on—and, hey, presto, I've got a bionic ear. I can hear the same as your mum and dad now—well, almost.'

'So you can't hear, like me?' Ruby asked, looking surprised.

'Nope. And it hasn't stopped me doing anything I want to do.' She laughed. 'Well, obviously I don't wear it if I go swimming. It'd be like putting your handheld game console in the bath.'

Ruby giggled. 'That'd be silly. It doesn't work if it gets wet.'

'Exactly.' Katrina smiled at her. 'So if your next test shows that you do need a hearing aid, you'll know not to worry because you'll be fine. And you can get special help at school if you need it.' She looked at Ruby's parents. 'There are support groups, and the audiology team can work with Ruby's school. And, believe me, a hearing aid takes a lot of the struggle out of lessons. There won't be any difference between Ruby and everyone else in her class.' She smiled at Ruby. 'Except you can show people exactly what the inside of your ear looks like and really gross them out. Oh, and you can choose your colour. I had to have a clear mould because I'm a grown-up, but you can have a pink sparkly one if you want.'

'Really?' Ruby's face brightened.

'Really. Or a purple one. I really wanted a bright blue one to match my eyes, but grown-ups don't get to have the fun ones.'

Rhys withdrew, feeling a complete and utter heel. Now he understood why Katrina had ignored him: she hadn't heard him. And because he'd called out from behind her she hadn't seen him either, so she'd had no idea he'd even spoken. Considering he'd been about to accuse her of deliberately ignoring him and being petty… Guilt flooded through him. Admittedly, he hadn't known Katrina Gregory for very long, but in that day and a half he'd really been aware of how warm and sweet she was. She wasn't the type to be petty or to bear grudges and give someone the silent treatment.

He really should stop judging people by his own family's behaviour.

And he most definitely owed Katrina an apology.

Katrina dropped by his office later that afternoon. 'I've got Petros Smith's blood results back. You're right—it's G6PD. Thanks for picking that up. There was something nagging in the back of my mind but I couldn't quite place it.'

'That's what colleagues are for,' he said lightly. 'Do you want me to come and talk to them with you?'

'No, that's fine. I can see you're busy.'

'If you're sure. The offer's there.' He paused. 'Actually, before you go, can you close the door a second?'

Her eyes narrowed. 'Why?'

'I'd like a quick word with you.'

She looked wary, but did as he asked. 'What is it?'

'Sit down. I'm not going to bite your head off. It's just…' He sighed. 'I owe you an apology.'

She blinked, but sat down. 'An apology? Why?'

'I called you earlier. On two separate occasions. You ignored me.'

She flushed. 'Sorry, I—'

'Let me finish,' he cut in. 'I thought it was deliberate, so I was going to ask you into my office for a quiet chat and sort out whatever the problem was. Then I overheard you talking to Ruby Jeffers and her parents—and I realise now you didn't hear me.'

She winced. 'Sorry. Sometimes it's difficult at work, especially in an open area—it gets a bit noisy and I have to rely on lip-reading a lot more than I do at home.'

'Don't apologise. You've done nothing wrong—but now I know about it, I'll make sure you're facing me and that I've got your attention before I talk if it's noisy.'

'Thank you.' She stood up. 'I'd better go and see the Smiths.'

He knew he should leave it there. They had a truce. But something seemed to take over his mouth, and he found himself saying, 'Before you do—would you have dinner with me this evening?'

She looked surprised. 'But you don't…'

'Don't what?'

'Don't do team nights out.'

'I'm not very good with crowds.' He rubbed a hand across his face. 'I'm not much of a drinker, I loathe karaoke and that sort of thing, and I'd rather go out for a good meal and a decent conversation than sit at the end of a huge table, not really knowing anyone and being only too aware that I was only invited because everyone's being polite and it's cramping their style having the consultant around.'

'I see.'

Her expression intrigued him. 'Why did you think I said no to team nights out?'

'You mean, when most new consultants would go on absolutely everything to try and bond with the team?' She spread her hands. 'No idea. Maybe you have a complicated home life.'

'There's just me,' he said softly. 'No ties of any sort. So it's pretty simple.'

'Well, thank you for asking me,' she said politely, 'but I'm afraid I'll have to pass. I don't believe in dating colleagues. If it doesn't work out, it makes life very awkward for everyone else on the ward.'

His brain registered her refusal—but her reason told him something else. She hadn't refused because she was already involved with someone else or because she wasn't interested in him: she'd refused because he was her colleague.

'You're right, it can make things difficult,' he agreed. He'd seen it happen with other people rather than experienced it himself; in the past, he'd dated people who worked in the same hospital, but never colleagues from his own ward. 'I'm asking you out to dinner because we've got off on the wrong foot and I'd like us to start again as colleagues—and it's a more civilised way of starting a good working relationship.'

'The wrong foot.' She pursed her mouth. 'You were telling me how to do my job yesterday.'

He'd wondered if she'd bring that up. 'I was concerned that you're getting too emotionally involved with your patients. That's not healthy for you *or* for the patient.' He smiled to soften his words. 'But I saw you telling a story in the playroom yesterday afternoon.'

'On my time, not the ward's time.' She folded her arms. 'And I assume you want me to stop?'

'No. Actually, I was thinking you'd be a natural as a teacher.'

Her face relaxed. 'My best friend from school's a primary school teacher. She uses a puppet to tell stories to her class and it works well, so I borrowed her idea for the ward.'

'And it's a good one. The children seemed to enjoy it.'

'Anything that makes hospital easier for them and reduces the stress on their parents means that they can spend their energy on getting well. And it helps the brothers and sisters, too.' She spread her hands. 'And I enjoy it. If we've had one of those days where everything's gone wrong, seeing the smiles on the faces of the little ones always makes me remember that life's good.'

'So you're a glass-half-full person?' he asked.

'Definitely.'

'Then have dinner with me tonight. As col-leagues—and potential friends,' he said.

She looked at him for a long, long moment. 'Not a date.'

'Not a date,' he confirmed. 'And you can choose where we go.'

'All right. Thank you. Do you want to go straight after work?'

'After,' he said, 'you've done your story.'

Her smile was the sweetest reward he could have asked for. 'I'll come and collect you, then. See you later.'

'See you later,' he said softly.

CHAPTER THREE

THIS wasn't a date, Katrina reminded herself as she walked from the playroom to Rhys's office. It was the beginning of a working relationship. And, as she'd told Madison, she was perfectly happy with her life the way it was.

She rapped on Rhys's open door and leaned against the doorjamb. 'Ready?'

He looked up from his computer. 'Can you give me three minutes while I save this file and switch off the computer?'

He was as good as his word, saving the file immediately, logging off then and switching off the machine. 'So where are we going?' he asked as he stood up.

'Do you like Moroccan food?'

'Yes.'

'Good. There's a really fabulous Moroccan

restaurant a couple of streets from here called Mezze—Maddie and I go there a lot.'

'Maddie? Ah, now I know why you looked familiar when I first met you. Madison Gregory in Maternity—she's your sister?'

'As good as, yes,' Katrina said. 'Technically, she's my cousin, but our dads have a family business and our mums are best friends, so we grew up together.' She laughed. 'Because she's two years older than I am, Maddie likes to point out that she's the *big* sister. Even though she's still shorter than I am when she's wearing spike heels and I'm barefoot, bless her.' She paused. 'What about you—do you have any brothers or sisters?'

'I'm an only child.'

His voice was neutral, but Katrina was used to watching faces and picking up visual clues to compensate for years of not quite being able to hear someone's tone. She was sure that Rhys was masking something. Though as they were still getting to know each other, now wasn't the time to push him to talk to her, the way she would have pushed Will or Tim or any of the nursing staff on the ward.

She kept the conversation light until they

reached Mezze. As they walked in, Rhys took in their surroundings—the rich saffron walls, the ruby and terracotta silk cushions, the tealight candles in stained-glass holders in the centre of the glass-topped tables. Katrina thought he looked as impressed as she'd felt when she and Madison had first discovered the restaurant.

'Good evening, Katrina. Your usual table?' the waiter asked.

'Thanks, Hassan. That'd be lovely.'

When they were settled at a table with menus and had ordered a sparkling mineral water, Rhys raised an eyebrow. 'I know you said you come here a lot…but the staff here actually know you by name?'

'I love Moroccan food,' she said simply. 'Maddie hates cooking, so we tend to come here most weeks. Either here, or there's a really fabulous pizzeria in the next street.'

'So you know the menu well.' His eyes took on a teasing glint. 'Or are you boring and pick the same thing each week?'

'I tend to choose the same pudding, I admit,' she said with a smile, 'but I've tried everything on the menu.' And there was a long, long list of dishes.

'So what do you recommend?'

Katrina leaned back against her chair. 'We could be boring, and order a starter each and a main course. Or…' She paused. 'We could order a huge pile of starters and share it like a *mezze*.'

He laughed. 'I can guess which you'd prefer. A huge pile of starters it is.'

She talked him through the menu and when Hassan brought their drinks over they were ready to order a selection.

'So tell me about yourself,' Katrina said when Hassan had gone.

Rhys shrugged. 'There's not much to tell. I'm Welsh—well, with a name like Rhys Morgan and my accent, that's pretty obvious. I grew up in South Wales, I trained in Cardiff and I moved to London just over three weeks ago.'

That didn't tell her much about him at all—his dreams, his passions in life—but before she had the chance to ask anything else, he said, 'Your turn.'

'I'm English, I grew up in Suffolk and I trained in London.' The same bare facts that he'd given her. Although maybe telling him more might encourage him to open up to her, she decided. 'I never wear pink—my cousin Maddie has the girly gene in the family—and I loathe the romantic comedies she insists on dragging me to.' She smiled wryly. 'She hates the kind of films I like. And going to an arthouse cinema on my own feels a bit...' She wrinkled her nose. 'Well, I prefer to go with someone so I can talk about the film afterwards. That's half the fun of a cinema trip.'

'What would you define as arthouse films?' he queried.

'This is where you can officially label me weird,' she said. 'Not modern ones—really old ones. Films like *Citizen Kane* and *Vertigo*. I have a bit of a soft spot for *film noir*.'

'Good choice,' he said. 'I really like the ones written by Cornell Woolrich as well as the Raymond Chandler films.'

She blinked, then fiddled with her hearing aid. 'Nope, it's working,' she said. 'Tell me—did I imagine it or did you really just say "Cornell Woolrich"?'

'I did.' He smiled. 'I've got all his short stories, too. I discovered them when I was a teenager and loved them—mind you, after one particular story it took me two years before I could order lamb again. And in a Welsh pub that's a bit difficult.'

She laughed, knowing exactly which story he meant—a tale with a twist that had had exactly the same effect on her. 'I think,' Katrina said, 'you and I are going to get on very well together.'

He lifted his glass. 'I'll drink to that.'

Her fingers brushed against his as they clinked glasses, and that same weird awareness she'd felt when she'd first shaken his hand seemed to fizz through her body.

An awareness she wasn't going to act on. She already knew first-hand what happened when you dated a colleague and it went wrong. The awkwardness of having to work together afterwards, trying not to think about just how intimately you knew each other. The embarrassment of everyone knowing what a failure your relationship was, thanks to the hospital grapevine. And, worse still, in a break-up as messy as hers had been with Pete, your colleagues on the ward feeling forced to take sides... No. She wasn't risking that happening ever again. Her relationship with Rhys was going to be a friendship—and nothing more.

Their food arrived, a huge platter containing little dishes and a heap of rustic bread.

'Lamb.' She gestured to the skewers of meat rubbed with spices and then chargrilled.

He laughed. 'That's a barefaced attempt to get me to leave it all for you to scoff.'

'Rats. My dastardly plan has been foiled,' she said, laughing and breaking off a piece of bread so she could scoop up some of the roast aubergine purée. 'Mmm. This is good.'

He tried the tabbouleh. 'So's this. Is that cinnamon I taste?'

'And watercress.' She paused. 'Is your palate honed that well by eating out a lot, or do you cook as well?'

'I eat out a fair bit,' he admitted. 'I can cook—but if I've worked late it's quicker and easier to stop somewhere on the way home.'

If? From what Lynne had said, it was more like 'when', she thought.

'How about you?' he asked.

'Cooking relaxes me. I like experimenting.' She smiled. 'And anything involving chocolate.'

He gestured to the table. 'No chocolate here.'

'Ah, but you wait until you try the chocolate

and cardamom ice cream from the dessert menu.'

As they worked their way through the little savoury pastries stuffed with cheese, the stuffed vine leaves and the felafel, Rhys asked, 'So how was little Petros Smith?'

Katrina wrinkled her nose. 'His haemoglobin levels weren't brilliant, but nowhere near bad enough to need a transfusion, and I think it would've been more stressful for him if I'd admitted him—so I let his mum take him home. I gave her a leaflet about Petros's condition and told her what to look out for; she's promised to bring him straight back to us if she's worried at all. He should pick up with a bit of rest—and the main thing is that his family knows now that there's a problem and what he needs to avoid in future.'

'That's good. What about the Jeffers family?'

'They're coming to terms with the situation,' Katrina said. 'They have another audiology appointment in six weeks' time, but they were warned this morning that Ruby's fairly likely to need an aid.' She smiled wryly. 'I wish health screening had been as good when I was a kid.'

Clearly Katrina had had hearing difficulties for a long time, Rhys thought. 'So how long have you been deaf?'

'I'm not profoundly deaf—it's moderate to severe hearing loss,' she explained. 'Looking back, it started when I was about seven, but nobody picked it up until Maddie was at med school and did a module on audiology. I was in my first year, she was in her third, and you know what it's like when you're a med student—you read up on symptoms and you spot them in yourself or other people.'

'Yes, I remember doing that myself,' he said with a smile.

'Anyway, she nagged me to go and get my hearing checked. She even came with me to the audiology department for moral support, bless her. And that's when we found out.'

'Why didn't anyone pick it up earlier?' he asked.

'I was a bit of a dreamer as a child—well, I still am, from time to time—so everyone thought I was just on Planet Katrina and wasn't listening.' She shrugged. 'And you know what it was like when we were young. They simply didn't do the kind of screening they do now.' She rolled her eyes. 'I say "we". I'm twenty-eight, and I assume you're not that much older than I am?'

'I'm thirty-two,' he confirmed. 'So it was a bit of a shock when you got the results?'

She nodded. 'All I could think of was that I was too young to be going deaf—that it was something that only happened to geriatrics.' She gave a mirthless laugh. 'And that's despite the fact that there were several children in the waiting room for the audiology test. I have to admit I was struggling a bit to hear in lectures, but I thought it was just the acoustics of the theatre—that the place was full so it swallowed up noise. You know, in the same way that empty tube trains are much noisier than ones that are stuffed with people in the rush hour.'

'So having an aid fitted made a difference?'

'And how.' Her face was suddenly animated. 'It was incredible. I discovered I could hear better from the back of the auditorium than I'd ever been able to do from the front. And the dawn chorus…I'd never been able to hear it before. Well, not that I remember, anyway. I drove everyone bananas for the first couple of months, wanting to know what each new sound was.' She smiled. 'I was really lucky and had one of the digital aids straight off—the microprocessor is programmed to fit my personal pattern of hearing loss. It's never going to be quite as good as having full hearing, I know, but it's made a big difference to me and I don't get so tired—I don't have to concentrate quite so hard talking to people, or rely on subtitles on a television screen.'

'I had no idea you had a hearing difficulty until I saw you take your hearing aid out and show Ruby,' he said.

'I suppose I should have told you.' She shrugged. 'But, then again, just because I can't hear that well, it doesn't mean I have to be treated differently.'

He blinked in surprise. 'Why on earth do you think I would have treated you differently?'

'Some people can be a bit funny about it when they find out. They start talking really loudly— as if that makes any difference—or they treat me as if I'm slow and can't understand what they're saying. Which, I have to admit, drives me crazy. If you talk to me and I'm not facing you, I don't always realise that you're talking to me and I might not pick it up, but otherwise I'm just your average person.'

Average? No, she wasn't just your average

person. There was something special about Katrina Gregory.

Rhys suppressed the thought as quickly as it arrived. He wasn't looking for a relationship. There wasn't room in his life.

'So I don't tend to tell people unless they notice,' she finished. 'It avoids the fuss.'

He could understand that. He didn't like fuss either. 'Do you know what caused your hearing loss?' he asked.

She nodded. 'I had a CT scan because there was a spike in the higher frequencies and they wanted to rule out anything nasty, like an acoustic neuroma.' She grinned. 'I asked if I could have a picture. I thought they'd print something on paper, but they actually gave me a film. It's fabulous. Maddie says I only did it so I could show everyone and prove that there was a brain in my head—but that's because I got higher marks in my exams than she did.'

Katrina's expression told him that this was mutual affectionate teasing rather than a bitchy swipe. Rhys found himself wondering what it would've been like to grow up with a sibling or close cousin teasing him like that.

His family didn't do teasing.

If the truth were told, they didn't do anything except avoid each other.

'I take it the scan was clear?' he asked.

'Yes. And after talking to me the registrar said he thought my hearing loss was probably caused when I had mumps as a child. Maddie still has the odd guilty fit about it, because she says she's the one who gave me mumps so therefore it's her fault I can't hear properly.' Katrina flapped a hand. 'But that's just *ridiculous*. She's also the one who gave me my hearing back, because if she hadn't nagged me about it I probably wouldn't have bothered getting a referral to audiology—I would've carried on as I was, assuming that I was completely normal because I didn't know any different, and struggling a bit more than I'd ever admit to because I didn't want to be treated differently.'

Rhys went very still. A child with a virus causing a serious condition. It was a little too close for comfort to his past. 'So your family blames Maddie for your hearing loss?' he asked.

'No, of course they don't!' She frowned. 'How on earth can you blame a child for falling ill? It's not Maddie's fault that she picked up a virus at school—the same as it wasn't my fault that I caught it too and it affected me in a different way to the way it affected her.' She shrugged. 'These things just happen. You can't let it ruin the rest of your life.'

These things just happen.

How very different his life might have been if his family had chosen that line of thought. If they'd been strong enough to pull together instead of letting his little sister's death tear them apart.

'Are you all right, Rhys?' she asked, looking slightly concerned.

'I'm fine.' You couldn't change the past, so in his view there was no point in talking about it. 'And you're right about this food. It's fabulous.'

Katrina realised that Rhys had deliberately changed the subject. Something was clearly wrong, but he didn't want to talk about it. Not here and now, at least. Maybe he'd open up to her when they got to know each other a little better.

They spent the rest of the evening talking about food and films and books, and Katrina was surprised by how much their tastes meshed. But it wasn't just that. There was something about Rhys. Something in his blue, blue eyes that made her heart beat a little bit faster and made her wonder what it would feel like if that beautiful mouth slid across her own. Which shocked her, as she hadn't wanted to kiss anyone—hadn't even *thought* of kissing anyone—since Pete. Hadn't thought of a man in terms of anything other than as a colleague for the last couple of years.

This was crazy.

Particularly as Rhys worked with her.

Been there, done that, worn the T-shirt to shreds. She certainly wasn't going to risk a repeat of what had happened with Pete—the horrendous atmosphere that had, in the end, forced her to move hospitals to get away from the awkwardness. She loved working at the London Victoria—really loved the way everyone on the ward was like a huge extended family. No way would she be stupid enough to forget that lesson now, have an affair with Rhys and end up having to leave here, too.

Finally, after hot sweet mint tea and tiny pastries soaked in honey, she leaned back in her chair. 'I'm almost too full to move.'

'You should've left me the lamb,' he said with a grin.

'Baa,' she retorted. Then she glanced at her watch. 'Do you know, we've been here three hours?' And yet it had felt like minutes.

'I'd better get the bill,' he said.

'No, we're going halves,' she protested.

'Absolutely not. This was my idea—my apology to you.'

'Ah, but we're friends now. And friends *share*.'

He folded his arms. 'Don't argue with me, Dr Gregory, or I'll pull rank.'

'Bossy, huh?' But she wasn't going to argue—she'd had much a better idea. 'Tell you what. You can pay this time, but next time's *my* bill. We can go and see a film in Leicester Square or something and talk about it over tapas afterwards.'

'That,' he said, 'would be lovely. I'd like that.'

After Rhys had paid the bill, he insisted on seeing Katrina home.

'There's no need, you know,' she said. 'I've lived in London for ten years now. I'm used to being independent.'

'Humour me. It's a Welsh thing.'

'So you're Sir Lancelot?' she teased.

'Lancelot was French. Gawain, on the other hand, was Welsh.'

She laughed. 'Oh, I can see I'm going to enjoy being friends with you, Rhys Morgan.'

He laughed back. 'So are you going to let me see you home?'

'If you insist. You could probably do with walking some of this food off, too,' she added cheekily.

They left the restaurant and walked through the back streets. Eventually, Katrina paused outside a small Victorian terraced house. 'This is mine. Would you like to come in for a coffee?' she asked.

Although Rhys knew it would be more sensible to refuse—things were already going fast enough to set alarm bells ringing in his head—at the same time he didn't want the evening to end just yet. 'Thanks. That'd be nice.'

'Good.' She unlocked the door, then ushered him into the sitting room. 'Take a seat. I'll be back in a moment.'

Katrina's house radiated calm. Pale walls, plants everywhere, and shelves of books and films. No music, though, he noticed. That was clearly one of the areas where he and Katrina differed. And that probably had much to do with her hearing.

There were framed photographs on the mantelpiece and he walked over to take a closer look. A picture of Katrina with her cousin at what was obviously Madison's graduation; another of Katrina in graduation robes with people who he assumed were her parents; another taken of Katrina, Madison and both sets of parents in a garden; more photographs of Katrina's parents. The warmth of the family relationship was so obvious that Rhys felt a twist of envy: it was the complete opposite from his own family background.

Though in the circumstances he couldn't blame his father for walking away and trying to find happiness elsewhere. And, given that she'd lost a child and her marriage had disintegrated, he couldn't blame his mother for the way she was either. As Rhys had grown up, he'd come to terms with the way things were. And he'd worked out that it was much, much easier to be self-sufficient and keep people close enough to be professional, but far enough away so there was no risk of losing them from his life and getting hurt.

It wasn't as if there was a gap in his life. He had a job he was good at, a job he really, really loved; he had his music and his books and his films to fill his spare moments; and that was all he needed. Becoming involved with Katrina Gregory would just complicate things. He needed to get them back on the right sort of footing—colleagues and acquaintances only—and fast.

Katrina, walking back into the living room with two mugs of coffee, noted the expression on Rhys's face. Polite but distant again. Where was the man who'd chatted with her in the Moroccan restaurant, who'd relaxed enough with her to tease her back and laugh with her?

'One black coffee,' she said.

'Thanks.' He gave her a polite smile.

She couldn't think of a single reason why he would suddenly be so reserved with her, not after the evening they'd shared. Knowing how easily a small communication lapse could turn into something huge, she decided to face it head-on. 'Rhys, is something wrong?'

'Wrong? No.'

'But you've gone quiet on me.'

'I've just realised how late it is. And I'm afraid I'm a lark rather than an owl.'

'Me, too,' she said. 'Which means I end up drinking huge amounts of coffee on team nights out to keep me awake.'

'Sounds like a good plan.'

She sighed inwardly. He was definitely back to being polite and reserved. And she couldn't think of a single thing to say without it sounding inane or babbling.

The silence stretched until it was almost painful. And then he drained his mug. 'Thank you for the coffee.'

'Thank you for the meal,' she said, equally politely. 'And I hope you weren't just being nice when you said about going to the cinema with me. It's so rare to find someone who likes the same sort of films I do.'

He looked torn, but then he shook his head. 'No, I meant it.'

'Good. Then maybe we can check the listings together tomorrow, see what's showing later in the week. If you're not busy, that is.'

'That'd be nice.' He stood up. 'Goodnight, Katrina.'

'Goodnight.' She saw him to the door. 'See you on the ward.'

And when she washed up their coffee mugs, she was frowning. What had made Rhys suddenly clam up on her like that? Unless… She swallowed as the memories came back. Unless Rhys had had time to think about things and took the same view as Pete had. That her hearing was going to be an issue.

She'd thought she'd learned from her mistakes— but it was beginning to look as if she hadn't.

CHAPTER FOUR

WHEN the going gets tough, Katrina thought, the tough get cooking. And as she was on a late shift the next day, she spent the morning at home baking brownies. Lots of them. The combined scents of chocolate and vanilla lifted her mood, and by the time she'd walked into work she was feeling a lot more serene.

She left a note on top of the tin in the staff-room, telling everyone to help themselves, and was about to head for the ward when Rhys walked in.

'Good morning,' he said.

'Morning.' She gave him a polite smile, reminding herself that she was going to keep it professional between them.

'What do you know about choanal atresia?' he asked.

'The nasal passage is blocked by bone or

tissue, so the baby can't breathe properly,' she recited. 'Has the neonatal unit asked us to look at a baby?'

He shook his head. 'We've got a little girl in, four months old—one of her nasal passages is blocked, which is why it's taken so long to diagnose her. But I noticed yesterday you're very good at reassuring parents. The Gillespies are pretty upset, and I could do with a calming influence. As in *you*.'

She blinked. 'So you're being friendly again this morning.'

He flushed, clearly aware of exactly what she meant. 'I'm sorry, Katrina. What can I say?'

'Well, it'd be nice to know if I did or said anything to upset you last night.'

'No, of course you didn't.' He raked a hand through his hair. 'I'm just not very good at this friendship business. I've always been a bit of a loner and I'm more used to dealing with people on a professional basis. And I guess I panicked a bit because I was more relaxed with you yesterday than I've been with anyone in a long, long time. I'm sorry.'

He was being honest with her. She could see

it in his face. And it must have been difficult for him to open up that much to her just now. 'Apology accepted.'

'Good. So, the Gillespies—walk this way, Dr Gregory,' he said, 'and I'll talk you through baby Rosanna's notes.'

By the time they reached the cubicle, she knew the full patient history. Rhys introduced them both to the Gillespies.

'Oh, she's gorgeous,' Katrina said, stroking the baby Rosanna's cheek and smiling at Mrs Gillespie. 'You must be so proud of her.'

'We are.' Mrs Gillespie bit her lip. 'But...'

'You're worried sick about the operation. Of course you are,' Katrina said. 'But you're in the best place. I've worked here ever since I qualified, and Will's a fantastic surgeon.'

'Obviously you'll have a chance to meet him and talk to him before the operation,' Rhys said, 'but as he's in Theatre at the moment and we'll be caring for Rosanna after her operation, I wanted to talk you through what's going to happen this afternoon and answer any questions you might have.'

'Thank you,' Mr Gillespie said quietly.

'Rosanna has a condition called choanal

atresia—what that means is her nasal passages are narrower than they should be and she can't breathe properly, because babies can't breathe through their mouths until they're about six months old. It's usually picked up just after a baby's born, but in Rosanna's case only one passage has narrowed so it's taken us a bit longer to realise there's a problem,' Rhys said.

'Is she going to be all right?' Mrs Gillespie asked.

'Absolutely. She'll have an operation to widen her nasal passages and Will can then put a little plastic tube called a stent up each nostril. They won't hurt her, and the stents will keep her nostrils open while her nose heals,' Rhys explained. 'They'll stick out just a tiny bit.'

'The surgeon will take the tubes out in about three months' time, and she'll be able to manage perfectly without them,' Katrina added.

'The operation takes about an hour,' Rhys continued. 'It's under a general anaesthetic, so you won't be able to be with her during the operation, but you're very welcome to wait here on the ward or in the coffee bar, and we'll come and find you as soon as Rosanna's out of Theatre so you can give her a cuddle.'

'We can touch her afterwards?' Mr Gillespie asked.

'Definitely—talk to her, cuddle her, hold her hand. She'll be hooked up to some monitors, which might look a bit scary, but they're there to help us look after her,' Katrina reassured him. 'We'll check her breathing, her heart rate and oxygen levels, and she'll have a drip in to give her pain relief, but over the next few days we won't need them. As soon as she's feeding well and gaining weight, and we've taught you how to keep the stents clean, you can take her home and carry on as normal.'

'About six weeks after the operation, the surgeon will give Rosanna a check-up—again under a general anaesthetic—to make sure her nasal passages are still wide enough for her to breathe properly,' Rhys said. 'If you're at all worried in the meantime, you can talk to your health visitor or your family doctor, or ring us here on the ward.'

Mrs Gillespie dragged in a breath. 'But she's going to be all right?'

'She doesn't have any other health problems, so she'll grow up able to lead a perfectly normal life,' Rhys reassured her.

'We've got a leaflet about the condition we

can let you have, just to ease your mind a bit,' Katrina offered.

'It's a lot to take in, and if someone else in the family asks you about it, it might be hard to remember everything we've said,' Rhys added. 'Is there anything else you'd like to ask us?'

'I don't think so,' Mrs Gillespie said, looking doubtful.

'If you think of something later, just have a word with one of the nurses and they'll come and get one of us,' Rhys said. 'Rosanna's going to be in excellent hands. And you'll find that feeding her is a lot easier when she can breathe properly through her nose again.'

'She's such a tiny scrap. All my friends' babies are getting huge—I thought I was doing something wrong.' Tears welled up in Mrs Gillespie's eyes.

Katrina took her hand. 'You weren't doing anything wrong at all. You did absolutely the best thing, talking to your health visitor about it instead of struggling on your own and worrying.'

'My mother-in-law said I should have weaned her ages ago, that's why she isn't growing and why she isn't sleeping through the night yet.'

'Absolutely not,' Rhys said. 'We don't recommend weaning any earlier than four months. Rosanna was finding it hard to feed because it was hard work for her; she's been eating little and often because it's been easier for her. And babies decide when they're going to sleep through the night—every baby's different.'

'Though that's made it harder for you,' Katrina added. 'When you've had a lot of broken nights, you're tired and everything feels much more of a struggle than it would if you'd had enough sleep. Things are going to be a lot better after today.'

Mrs Gillespie brushed away a tear. 'Thank you. Sorry, I'm being stupid,' she said shakily.

'Not at all. You're human, and you've had a lot on your plate.' Katrina gave her a hug. 'Would you like me to get you some water or something?'

Mrs Gillespie shook her head. 'I'm all right. But thank you.'

'We'll come and see you again later,' Rhys promised. 'If you need anything, just ask. You're not making a nuisance of yourself—it's what we're here for.'

The Gillespies, clearly still overwhelmed, just nodded, and Rhys shepherded Katrina out of the cubicle. 'You,' he said, 'were brilliant. Thanks for your help.'

She shrugged. 'It's my job.'

'That's not how it comes across. You really care.'

'It's hard enough for parents to come to terms with the fact their baby's not well or needs an operation—the least we can do is make it easier for them. And Will's always taught the staff on this ward to treat patients as if they're our own family—so we show them respect, dignity and kindness.'

'Not all families are like that,' Rhys said.

That, Katrina thought, sounded personal. Not that she was going to try to get him to talk about it. She knew he'd only back away from her again. 'This one is,' she said simply. 'That's why I love working here so much.'

Later that afternoon, Katrina was having a coffee break when Rhys walked into the staffroom.

'Just the person I wanted to see,' she said with a smile.

'You want a second opinion on a patient?' he asked.

She shook her head. 'I've been looking at the

listings. There's a film festival on this week—and there are some really good ones showing tomorrow evening. Shall I book tickets for us?'

'Tomorrow evening?' He looked regretful. 'Sorry. No can do. I'm absolutely up to my eyes in paperwork. If I don't get some of it shifted…'

Katrina had the nasty feeling that he was making a polite excuse. Rhys's predecessor had been a little bit slapdash when it came to paperwork, but things couldn't be that bad, surely?

Well, she wasn't going to push herself in where she clearly wasn't wanted. 'I understand,' she said. Her mistake, thinking a shared love of film would be the basis of a good friendship. She could accept that he didn't want to be more than friends—that suited her, too—but it was obvious that Rhys wasn't interested in even that. 'And I'd better get on,' she said, glancing at her watch.

'You're not finishing your coffee?'

No. Knowing that she'd just made a fool of herself, she wanted to get out of there as fast as possible. Not that she was going to tell him that. 'I've already had too much caffeine today. I don't want to be still awake at 3:00 a.m.,' she said lightly, then rinsed out her mug and left the room.

She managed to keep a lid on her feelings until Friday evening, when she was leaving the ward after a late shift. The light was still on in Rhys's office; she knew he'd been in early and he should've gone home hours ago.

She rapped on the open door and he looked up. 'Yes?'

'Are you OK?' she asked.

'Fine.' He spread his hands. 'Why shouldn't I be?'

'It's just…' Even though part of her knew she should keep her mouth shut, the words spilled out. 'Apart from Tuesday, you've worked late every night this week, even if you came on duty well before 9:00 a.m.'

He shrugged. 'I'd rather spend my shifts actually treating patients on the ward or in clinic, and I need to catch up on the paperwork at some point.'

'Fair enough, but you're taking it to extremes. Working these sorts of hours really isn't good for you.'

He folded his arms and leaned back in his chair. 'So what are you saying, Katrina?'

'There's more to life than work, and maybe you should cut yourself some slack.'

'Thank you for your concern, but it's really not necessary.'

Her mouth really didn't know when to stop. 'Actually, I think it is. Because you're working ridiculous hours, everyone else is starting to feel they ought to work late, too—and that's not fair. Especially on colleagues who have young families.'

His expression was unreadable. 'I wasn't aware I'd asked anyone else to work late.'

'You haven't,' she admitted, feeling her face heat. 'But you do it, so they feel that if they don't they're not pulling their weight.'

'As you're clearly their spokesperson, you can go back and tell them I said I don't expect them to work the same hours as I do. If anyone has a problem with my hours, they can talk to me themselves.' He frowned. 'And if you'll excuse me, I need to go and check on a patient.'

'The night staff are perfectly capable of dealing with things. If there's a problem where they need your help, they'd be straight in to see you, and you know it.' She folded her arms. 'I think you're just avoiding the issue.'

'There isn't an issue.'

'Yes, there is. You're working crazy hours and it isn't good for you—or for the patients.' She shook her head in frustration. 'You have to be tired. Nobody can put in that amount of hours without wearing themselves out.'

'I'm fine. And, just for the record, I would never, *never* put a patient at risk.' His voice was very cool.

She sighed. 'You really won't let anyone close, will you? On Tuesday, you said we were friends. Since then, you've avoided me—and you've used work as an excuse not to go to the cinema with me. My mistake for taking your words at face value. You were obviously just being polite at the restaurant.'

When he said nothing, she shrugged. 'Well, now I know. I'll leave you to it. Sorry to have bothered you.' She turned away.

'Katrina, wait.' Rhys left his desk and put his hand on her shoulder as she reached the doorway.

She turned to face him. 'What?'

'I have the social skills of a rhinoceros. I'm fine with patients and their parents because it's work and I know what I'm doing. But...' He removed his hand from her shoulder and raked it through his hair. 'I'm not particularly good at this friendship stuff. I'm sorry.'

Katrina had known several people at university who had been practically geniuses in the lab, but utterly hopeless in social situations and hadn't had a clue what to say in the bar. Rhys was clearly the same type: talk about facts and food and film and medicine and he was fine. Talk about something personal, and he was all at sea. And right at that moment he was looking awkward and as embarrassed as she'd just felt. He was trying, really trying, at something he obviously found difficult. The least she could do was acknowledge that. 'Apology accepted.'

'I probably do put in too many hours. But I happen to like my job.'

'Including paperwork?' Now, that one she didn't believe.

'It's not quite the kind of paperwork you're thinking of. Right now I'm reviewing all our patient leaflets and updating them, and working out how we can make our department's website pages easier for parents and children to use. I could do it at home, but from a technical viewpoint it's a lot quicker to do it at the hospital. And,' he added, 'I might point out that you stay late, too, or you come in early to read stories to the children.'

'Half an hour at the beginning or end of my shift,' she said. 'That's reasonable. What you're doing *isn't* reasonable. It's practically doing a double shift. And don't protest, Rhys—you know it isn't reasonable.'

'So I'm a workaholic.' He spread his hands. 'It's not a crime. Plenty of other people work as hard as I do.'

She flushed. 'I'm not nagging.'

'Actually, you are.' He smiled ruefully. 'But I suppose you have a point. All right.' He glanced at his watch. 'Do you have to be somewhere, or do you fancy going for a drink?'

He was asking her out?

Her thoughts must have shown on her face, because he raised an eyebrow. 'As colleagues.'

'And then you'll blank me on Monday morning?' she asked wryly.

He sighed. 'I'll try not to. So. Do you want to go for a drink?'

'Thanks, but at this time of night everywhere's

going to be crowded and noisy.' She wrinkled her nose. 'Not to mention dark.'

'Which means it'll be difficult for you to hear or lip-read.' He grimaced. 'I'm sorry. I didn't think.'

She shrugged. 'Not your problem. But thanks for the offer, anyway. It was nice of you to ask.' And even though she was tempted—severely tempted—she didn't suggest an alternative. Because it would be all too easy to let herself fall for Rhys Morgan, to want something from him that he clearly wasn't prepared to give. 'I'd better be going. Have a nice weekend.'

'You, too.'

CHAPTER FIVE

Rhys was polite and pleasant over the following couple of weeks, treating Katrina just the same as his other colleagues. But Katrina found herself looking at his mouth when he talked, and not just to read his lips—half the time her attention strayed and she found herself wondering what it would be like to feel his mouth travelling along her skin. Every time her hand brushed against his, she felt that weird prickle of awareness down her spine, and the feeling grew stronger every single time.

Oh, lord. She should know better. Somehow she had to stop that weird, flipping-over sensation in the area of her heart every time she looked at him.

The worst thing was, she was pretty sure it was the same for him. Because she'd seen him looking at her mouth, too. She'd noticed his colour heighten when his hand brushed against hers—and she'd seen the way his eyes widened for just a fraction of a second and his mouth parted very, very slightly.

Signs of attraction. Of arousal.

And whenever she thought about it her temperature went up another notch.

Katrina was beginning to think that not acting on that mutual attraction was going to make life just as difficult as if they gave in to it and had an affair. And even though it was going to be awkward and embarrassing, she was going to have to talk to him about it. Be honest. And see if he had any better and more sensible ideas than the ones that were running through her own head.

She managed to keep her mind on her work—just—when she was talking to young Kevin Lacey and his mum. Though it really didn't help that Mrs Lacey had a very soft voice, and kept her head bowed so her hair fell in her face and obscured Katrina's view of her mouth.

Oh, lord.

She couldn't hear a single one of Mrs Lacey's questions, and she really wasn't sure that either Kevin or Mrs Lacey had taken in what she'd been saying about Kevin's condition and the operation he was going to have the following day.

Katrina definitely looked strained, Rhys thought. Which was unusual: normally she was brilliant with parents, relaxed and comforting. And although young Kevin Lacey had a serious condition, it was one that could be controlled rather than something terminal, so it wasn't one of those conversations where you knew the parents' hearts were breaking and you felt completely helpless and wondered what use all those years of training were.

A second look made him guess what the problem was: Katrina couldn't see Mrs Lacey's face to lip-read. The lunch trolley was coming round, so the ward was at its noisiest, with cutlery scraping against plates and everyone raising their voices correspondingly. Katrina must be really struggling to hear, he thought, especially if Mrs Lacey's voice was particularly quiet—and, judging by her body language, he rather thought it was.

He walked over to them. 'Hello. I'm Dr Morgan. How are you doing, Kevin?'

'All right,' Kevin replied bravely, through from his pallor and the way the child was wincing Rhys realised that he was far from all right. Clearly his enlarged spleen was causing him pain.

'Mrs Lacey?'

'Dr Gregory's being very helpful,' Mrs Lacey said.

He could barely catch what Mrs Lacey was saying, and his hearing was perfect. So, even with the hearing aid, Katrina didn't stand a chance. Not that he'd bring up her deafness, particularly in front of a patient or parent: he knew she was sensitive about it. But there was something he could do to make things easier for her. 'It's pretty noisy out here because it's lunchtime,' he said, 'and I know you must have a lot of questions about Kevin's condition and his operation tomorrow. Dr Gregory, I'm on a break now. Would you like to use my office so you've got somewhere a little quieter and less distracting to run through all the procedures with Mrs Lacey?'

The relief in her eyes made him sure he'd done the right thing. 'Thank you, Dr Morgan. That'd be good.'

He smiled back at her. 'My pleasure. I'll be back on the ward in half an hour or so, but take all the time you need. And if anyone needs me, they can bleep me.'

'I'll pass the message on to Lynne,' she promised.

'See you later,' he said, and left the ward.

'Would you like a sandwich or anything, Kevin?' Katrina asked. 'Dr Morgan won't mind if you have a snack or a drink in his office.'

He shook his head. 'Hurts too much.'

'I think you need more pain relief. When did you last give him paracetamol, Mrs Lacey?'

The woman whispered something Katrina didn't catch.

'I'm sorry, Mrs Lacey, it's really noisy out here and I can't hear you properly. Let's go to Dr Morgan's office.' Once she'd established that it had been four hours since Kevin had had any pain relief, she was able to give him more and wrote it up in the notes. She also made sure that both Mrs Lacey and Kevin had a drink, although both refused food.

'It's quite a lot to take in,' she said, 'so I'll go

over it all again, if that's all right with you. Kevin's got a form of anaemia called spherocytosis—what that means is that his red blood cells don't have their normal covering to hold them in shape and they become sphere-shaped.' She drew a quick sketch on the whiteboard by Rhys's desk to show them the difference between a normal blood cell and Kevin's. 'Because of their shape, the spleen decides they're abnormal and destroys them too early—that's why Kevin's pale and gets really tired after exercise. It also makes the spleen grow more than normal, which is why you're getting the pains in your tummy, Kevin.'

'And it will all go away when the doctor takes my spleen out?'

Clearly the little boy had been listening. She smiled at him. 'You'll stop being tired and you won't have the tummy pains, though unfortunately it won't make your red blood cells go back to normal.'

'And then he'll be all right?' Mrs Lacey asked.

This time, Katrina was able to hear her. 'Removing the spleen does cause some problems,' she said. 'Without a spleen you're more likely to pick up infections. Kevin will need to take antibiotics for the rest of his life to help avoid infections, and you need to make sure he gets vaccinated. I can give you a leaflet which will help you spot any signs of infection—if you see them, you need to take him to your GP straight away. He'll also need to carry a card with him at all times to say he has no spleen; then if he has to go into hospital or needs treatment the medical staff will know what to do.'

'So will it hurt, having the operation?' Kevin asked.

'You'll be asleep,' Katrina said, 'though you might feel a bit sick and dizzy or have a sore throat when you come round from the anaesthetic. It won't last long, though. It's going to be a bit more scary for your mum—we'll need to put a tube in from your nose to your tummy in case you don't feel like eating or drinking at first, and you'll also have a drip to give you pain relief.'

'Does the operation take long?' Mrs Lacey asked.

'Somewhere between ninety minutes and three hours,' Katrina said. 'You'll be able to stay with him until he's had the anaesthetic, and there are plenty of places where you can have a cup of coffee while you're waiting. He'll be able to go home in about a week, and because the stitches will dissolve on their own he won't need to come back to have them removed.' She smiled at Kevin. 'You'll be back to school in a month— but I'm afraid no sport for the next three months.'

'No football? But…' He looked dismayed. 'But I have to play. I'm in the school team.'

'Sorry, sweetheart. You need time to heal,' Katrina said. 'But I bet you you'll be able to play even better after the operation than you do now, because you won't get so tired.' She smiled at Mrs Lacey. 'Now, I'll get the surgeon and an-aesthetist to come and have a word with you later this afternoon, and they'll be able to answer any detailed questions you might have about the procedure. But if there's anything else you want to know, no matter how small it might seem, I'm here to help.'

'No football for three months.' Kevin's lower lip wobbled.

'It'll go by really quickly,' Katrina said. 'What with Bonfire Night and Christmas coming up, you'll be ready to play again before you know it.'

She answered Mrs Lacey's final questions, then shepherded them back out to the ward and sweet-talked Hannah, the auxiliary nurse, into finding Kevin a sandwich—with the pain under control again the little boy had recovered his appetite.

Katrina didn't see Rhys again until the end of her afternoon clinic. 'Thanks for rescuing me earlier,' she said. 'I really appreciate it.'

'No problem. I could barely hear her myself—the ward isn't exactly a quiet place, and if someone keeps their face covered you can't lip-read.'

Katrina grimaced. 'I should've said something.'

'Not necessarily.' Rhys frowned. 'I'm pulling rank. Come on. Coffee.'

'But I have paperwork to do,' she protested.

'Paperwork can wait. You've finished your clinic and I've done the ward rounds—it's time to take a break.'

'Rhys—' she began.

'I want to talk to you about something,' he said.

He wanted to talk to her? Her heart missed a

beat—and then she berated herself silently. Of course he didn't want to talk to her about their relationship. They didn't *have* a relationship, other than that of colleagues.

But she let him shepherd her to a quiet corner of the hospital canteen and buy her a latte.

'It's noisy enough in here for people not to be able to overhear us, but is it too noisy for you? Can you hear me OK?' he asked.

He'd automatically sat so his face was in the light; despite the hubbub around them she knew she'd be able to lip-read anything that she missed hearing. 'Yes.'

'Right. Now, I'm going to tell you something important, so I want you to pay attention. Katrina Gregory, you're a damn good doctor. And your hearing doesn't change that at all.'

She dragged in a breath. 'It's just that some-times… No, forget it.'

'Talk to me, Katrina,' he said.

She smiled wryly. 'Isn't that a bit like pots and kettles?'

He acknowledged her point with a smile of his own. 'People who keep themselves to themselves probably notice it more in other people. You need to talk about this.'

'As I said, pots and kettles.'

He flipped a hand dismissively. 'My personal life isn't spilling over into work.'

Katrina lifted her chin. 'Neither is mine.'

'I didn't mean that.' He sighed. 'I'm making a mess of this. What I'm trying to say is that I get the feeling you're worried about your hearing affecting your work—but from my point of view it doesn't. At all. You're good with the children and you're good with the parents. This afternoon, *anyone* would've found it difficult to hear Mrs Lacey. I couldn't hear her either. So it wasn't *you*.' He frowned. 'Has someone said something to you about it?'

'Not here.' The words were out before she could stop them.

His frown deepened. 'Do you mean you don't want to talk about it here, or that someone's said something to you elsewhere?'

She squirmed. 'Do we have to discuss this?'

'Yes. It's important. Katrina, nobody can overhear us,' he reassured her. 'And if someone's said something to upset you, I want to know.'

'It's in the past. I'm over it.'

'Are you?'

She lifted her chin. 'I don't mope about things.'

'I realise that, but if someone knocks your confidence, whatever they said comes back into your mind when you have a not-so-good day—like the one I think you've had today. You wouldn't be human if it was otherwise.'

'No.'

'So talk to me. It'll help.' He reached over and squeezed her hand. Just for a moment. And the need that surged through her took her breath away.

'Katrina?' he prompted.

'All right. Since you must know, it was my ex,' she said. 'Pete. Maddie calls him "Pete the Toad"—actually, that's her politest name for him.' She swallowed hard. She may as well tell Rhys the truth. And then he'd back off and she'd be able to get control of her emotions again. 'He left me because I was damaged goods. Because he was afraid that if he stayed with me and we got married and had a child, I wouldn't hear the baby crying—that I wouldn't be a good enough wife and I sure as hell wouldn't be a good enough mother.'

Rhys looked shocked. 'What? That's ridiculous. Katrina, look at the way you are with the kids on the ward. You're the one we rely on to calm kids down and tell stories and distract them, and you're an excellent doctor, too. Pete didn't have a clue what he was talking about.'

'No? We worked together. I was the SHO and he was the registrar on the children's ward.'

'Here?' he questioned. 'So it was the guy who was consultant before me?'

'No. Different hospitals. I moved here a couple of years back.' She dragged in a breath. 'Everyone knew what had happened when we split up. And it was awful, Rhys. The atmosphere on the ward was terrible. Nearly everyone took my side, apart from this one woman who… Well, it turned out she fancied Pete and thought that if she took his part he might, um, show some interest in her.'

'It sounds as if they deserved each other,' Rhys said.

'Probably. I have no idea if they got together or not and I really don't care. But I hated going into the ward every day and facing everyone. People were sympathetic, even kind, but I could see the pity in their eyes, and I loathed the fact they saw me as "poor Katrina" instead of who I am. By the end, I wasn't sure if they pitied me for the way Pete behaved or because I can't hear. And working with Pete was just sheer torture. I never want to be in that situation again.' She grimaced. 'It was so hard to face him, when I'd loved him so much and he'd rejected me. It made me start thinking that I was as useless as he said I was—useless at my job as well as my personal life. Everyone said that he was in the wrong, not me, but it made me question my judgement in men. If he was that awful, why had I been stupid enough to fall for him in the first place? Next time round, would I pick someone who'd treat me just as badly?'

'Useless? *You?* I know violence doesn't solve anything, but right now I'd love to break the guy's jaw,' Rhys said through gritted teeth. 'It's not true, Katrina. You're *not* damaged goods and you're very, very far from useless. You're kind and you're clever and you're a damned good doctor and you make the world a brighter place. Don't ever, *ever* think otherwise.'

The expression on his face told her he meant it. That he was livid with Pete on her behalf.

If he could feel that protective towards her, that had to mean something. And the way he'd looked at her over the last couple of weeks…she was pretty sure he felt the same way that she did. Longing. Attraction.

But she couldn't act on it.

She had to explain—but, then again, how could she? It wasn't an easy subject to broach— and Rhys was such a private man, it made things even more difficult. She swallowed hard. 'Rhys. I don't… Look, this is awkward.'

'I'm not going to betray any confidences, if that's what you're worrying about. What you just told me stays with me and only me.'

She could feel the colour flooding into her face. 'Thank you. But Pete…that's why I never want to date a colleague again. I don't want to go through that horrible mess when it's over, of people taking sides and talking about me, even if they mean well.'

'Perfectly understandable. I'd feel the same.'

'Is that what happened to you, too?'

She'd told him a confidence. Something she clearly didn't talk about very much. And right

now Rhys could tell that Katrina felt really vul-
nerable. The only way he could think of to ease
that was to tell her a confidence in return. 'Not
exactly. I never dated anyone on the same ward.
But…' He paused. 'This is the same deal. What
I tell you stays with you and only you.'

'Of course.'

'My parents split up when I'd barely started
school. I don't want to go into details, but it was
pretty messy, and I promised myself I'd never let
that happen to me.' He smiled wryly. 'Of course,
when I grew up, I realised that marriage doesn't
necessarily end in divorce—not everyone's from
a broken home.'

'My parents have been married for thirty years,'
Katrina said. 'And they can act embarrassingly
like teenagers—Maddie's parents are the same.'

'They're the lucky ones.' He shrugged. 'As I
said, I realise that relationships can work—but
mine don't tend to. I've tried to make a go of
things with other relationships. But it's never
worked out in the end.'

'Is that a warning?' she asked.

'No, it's a statement of fact. Even though I
know the odds are probably on my side, I

suppose emotionally I'm not prepared to take the risk. Which is probably why I keep people at a distance because it's a hell of a lot easier that way. Less stressful. Work, I can deal with. Personal stuff...' He propped his elbows on the table and rested his chin on his clasped hands. 'Can I be honest with you?'

She nodded.

'I'm attracted to you, Katrina. Very attracted. I haven't felt like this about anyone since...' He shook his head. 'Since I don't know when. Though I'm not going to do anything about it because I agree with you that relationships between colleagues are a bad idea. But, just so we're clear on this, I want you to know that your hearing difficulty has absolutely nothing to do with why I'm not going to ask you out. It's part of you, and I think because of it you're more aware of other people's feelings. You read body language better than anyone else I've ever met, so no doubt you've already guessed what I was going to say.'

'I did wonder.' She bit her lip. 'And you're perceptive. You saw when I was struggling today and you sorted it out without making me feel stupid, the way Pete did.'

'Stupid?' Rhys blinked. 'What the hell was wrong with the man? You're not stupid. You're practically ready to be registrar now. You'll ace your exams.'

'I hope so.'

'I *know* so,' Rhys said, taking her hand again and squeezing it.

She licked her lower lip and it set his pulse racing.

'Don't do that,' he begged, releasing her hand.

'Do what?'

'Lick your lip like that. Because it makes me want to…' He dragged in a breath. 'It makes me want to kiss you. And, quite apart from the fact I'm trying to stay away from you, we're in the middle of the hospital canteen. If I do what I really want to do right now, the rumour mill will zip into action so fast it'll practically explode.' He forced himself to take a sip of his coffee, but the cup clattered against the saucer as he returned it. 'You could have me on a harassment charge for admitting that.'

She shook her head. 'Like I said, you're perceptive. So you must have guessed it's the same for me. Right from when I first met you.' She raked a hand through her hair. 'I can't take that chance either, Rhys. I can't risk it all going wrong—I love it here and it'd break my heart if I had to leave, the way I did in my last job.'

'I'm not Pete, so it wouldn't come to that,' he said, 'but you're right. We can't do this. Because you deserve the kind of happiness I don't think I could give you. I mean, sure, we could have a wild affair.' It was a mistake, putting it into words: he could already feel his body's reaction to the idea of making love with her, and the way Katrina's pupils dilated slightly told him that it was the same for her.

Oh, lord.

He needed to get some control here. And fast.

'But I'm not looking for marriage and a future,' he continued, 'and it's not fair of me to ask you to give up the chance of meeting someone who can offer you what you want.'

'So where do we go from here?' she asked.

'We stay as we are. Colleagues. We're both strong enough to put our careers and our patients first.'

'And that's the right thing to do. The sensible thing,' Katrina agreed.

102 THE CHILDREN'S DOCTOR'S SPECIAL PROPOSAL

'Good. So we're clear on that.'

'We're clear,' she agreed.

He should have been relieved. But he wished things could have been different. 'When we've finished our coffee, we'll go back to the ward. You go your way, I'll go mine. We work together. And eventually we'll both get over this blip and we'll be able to look at each other without…'

'Wanting to rip each other's clothes off?' she suggested.

He groaned. 'I think I should've ordered a cold shower with that coffee. But, yes. That's what I mean. And I know I've already said it, but I think it bears repeating: just so you know, this has absolutely nothing to do with your hearing.'

'Thank you,' she said solemnly. 'I appreciate it.'

He was still angry on her behalf. Her ex had really done a number on her. Part of him wanted to kiss her better, to show her just how desirable she was. But then they'd end up with a complication they could both do without. Katrina deserved to find happiness with someone who could give her what she needed—which ruled him out.

Right now, they had a deal. And he had every intention of sticking to it. No matter what his body thought.

CHAPTER SIX

THEY managed to keep things on an even keel for the next few weeks—though Katrina knew the second that Rhys walked into the room, even if her back was turned and she couldn't hear him, and she was pretty sure it was the same for him, too. The awareness. The longing. The wondering.

We could have a wild affair. His words echoed in her head. Maybe they should. Maybe it would get things out of their system and then they could go back to being colleagues.

Or maybe it would just make things worse—because although she could imagine what it would be like to kiss Rhys, to make love with him, the reality would be even more intense. Something she wouldn't want to give up.

She was going to have to start taking long, cold showers. Or doing a few lengths of the local pool—which was always freezing—before work.

She was still thinking about it when she saw Rhys walk into the department, carrying a rolled-up sleeping bag and a suitcase.

Was he going away somewhere straight after work? As far as she knew, he wasn't off duty the next day. Odd. It didn't make sense.

Until she walked into the staffroom during her break and saw him ending a call on his mobile phone and crossing something off a list.

'Everything OK?' she asked.

'In a word, no.' He rolled his eyes. 'You know that storm we had last week? It took some tiles off my roof, and my landlord sent someone round to fix it—except they found some asbestos. I have to move out while it's being fixed. And because the landlord's panicking about health and safety, that means today.'

She glanced at his list—a printout of local hotels and their phone numbers. Most of them were crossed through. 'No luck finding anywhere?'

'Everywhere's fully booked, with it being Bonfire Night, half-term and then that big charity concert at the end of the week.' He sighed. 'I have a feeling I'm going to be sleeping in my office for a few nights. That's why I brought my sleeping bag in.'

'Rhys, you can't. I mean…I know there are showers and what have you at the hospital, but living out of a suitcase would be awful. And you won't get much rest.'

'It's not ideal, I admit,' he said, 'but I can rough it for a few days.'

Her mouth went into gear a moment before her brain did. 'Look, I have a spare bedroom. Why don't you come and stay with me?'

He blinked. 'Katrina, that's really generous of you—but I can't possibly put you out like that. I have no idea how long it's going to take to sort out my flat. It could be days, it could be weeks.'

'It's not a problem.' Apart from the fact that they'd been trying to stay apart. But they'd managed it so far. If they could do it at work, they could do it outside work, surely? And she couldn't see him in a hole like this. She would've made the same offer to any of her colleagues.

'Then thanks—I owe you one,' Rhys said.

'So that suitcase and the sleeping bag is all you've got?'

'I don't travel *quite* that light.' He smiled wryly. 'I have a flat full of books and films. But at least the place is furnished, so it's only a couple of carloads.'

Her mouth was really on a roll. 'I'll give you a hand. If I drive over to your place this evening, we can load my car up as well as yours and it'll only take one trip.'

'Katrina, you're putting me up. I can hardly ask you to do all that lugging about as well.'

'It isn't a problem. Anyone here would do the same—you help each other out if you're stuck.'

'Then thanks. I really appreciate this, Katrina. And I'll buy us a take-away tonight,' he promised.

'You're on.' She smiled. 'Pizza, salad and the nicest rosemary flatbread in the world.'

'That,' he said, 'is a deal.'

After work, Rhys made two quick stops on the way home, stored one of his purchases in the passenger footwell of his car, then took the packing tape indoors and retrieved the flat-packed removal boxes from underneath his bed. He'd made up the boxes and packed the rest of his clothes by the time Katrina rang the doorbell.

'Come in. Coffee?' he asked, ushering her inside.

'Thanks.'

He quickly went into the kitchen and switched on the kettle. 'I've emptied my bedroom and the bathroom. It's just the kitchen and living room to do now.' He smiled. 'I'm glad I moved most of my music over to a hard disk system a couple of years back, or it'd take twice as long to pack.' And he'd only unpacked a small proportion of his sheet music in the first place, which helped.

Her eyes widened as she saw his cello case and the music stand in the living room. 'I would've guessed that you can sing well, being Welsh, but I had no idea you played an instrument.'

He laughed, disassembling the music stand and putting it on top of the sheet music. 'Don't believe the stereotype—not every Welshman can sing. School assemblies used to be torture, with half the kids singing out of tune.'

'Have you been playing for very long?' she asked.

'We always had a piano and I used to bang the keys when I was a toddler. I started proper lessons when I was, what, three and a half.' Before everything had gone wrong. And afterwards he'd found he was happiest when he was playing music. Filling the silence in the house. 'Later I learned to play the cello as well.'

She glanced round. 'You don't have a piano now?'

'Not any more. It's not quite as portable as a cello,' he said wryly. 'Though I admit I miss the piano. When I get round to buying a place in London, the first thing I'm going to do is buy myself a piano.'

'So you left your piano back in Wales?'

'Moving it was going to be a hassle—I didn't know if there'd be room in a rented place or how long I'd end up in a chain if I bought somewhere of my own. My colleague's daughter wanted to learn, and they're friends so I gave it to them.' It had been a wrench, but at least he'd known his piano would have a good home and be looked after.

'Nobody in our family plays an instrument,' Katrina said. 'Dad and Uncle Bryan always have music on in the garage, and Maddie's really into 1950s stuff—Dean Martin and Julie London and soft jazz—but none of them do anything more than sing along and dance around the place.'

Remembering the absence of music in Katrina's living room, Rhys had a feeling that she didn't join in. Unless she, too, kept all her music as digital files…but somehow he didn't think she did. 'What about you?' he asked.

She wrinkled her nose. 'I normally go along with the kind of stuff everyone else likes. I don't tend to bother with having the radio or what have you on in the house, or if I'm driving somewhere on my own.'

So his guess had been right. 'Maybe,' he said, 'I can introduce you to the stuff I like. Though I should warn you it's classical, rather than pop or rock.'

'I'm not sure I'll be able to appreciate it that well,' she said, 'but thanks for the offer.'

Of course. She'd said that she had a problem with high-frequency sounds; she might have a problem at the lower end of the scale, too.

'So shall I start with the films?' she asked. 'Any particular order?'

'Just however you can fit them into the boxes,' he said. 'I'll start on the books.'

'So did you ever think about becoming a professional musician?' she asked.

'Sort of. I almost studied music instead of medicine. It was a pretty hard choice to make.'

'What made you pick medicine in the end?'

'I wanted to make people better,' he said simply. 'Though my music teacher was pretty upset with me.'

'You have to follow your heart. And you can still play for pleasure.'

'That's what I said to her. And paediatrics is really rewarding.' He shrugged. 'So I know I made the right choice.'

It didn't take long to finish packing Rhys's books and films. He refused to let Katrina carry anything heavier than the briefcase containing his laptop, so he packed the boxes and cases into both cars while she finished putting his kitchen things into a box.

And one thing she'd really noticed about his flat was the lack of personal things. Sure, he had books and films, but there was nothing to give a clue to Rhys the man. There hadn't been a single photograph on his shelves or mantelpiece. No postcards held on to the fridge with magnets. Nothing personal at all.

She knew he was an only child and his parents had split up when he'd been young, but she'd expected to see a picture of at least one of his parents in a frame, like she had on her own mantelpiece. Or maybe a shot of a much-loved family pet. Or even one of Rhys as a student, in the middle of a group of friends.

He'd warned her that he kept people at a distance. He had said that he'd given his piano away to a colleague and friend, she remembered. So he was obviously able to connect with people.

Nevertheless, she'd never met anyone quite so self-contained as Rhys Morgan, and she had the distinct impression that she would barely know she had anyone staying in her home while he was there. Which, in a way, would be a good thing—it removed temptation. Part of her thought it was a seriously bad idea, offering Rhys a place to stay when she knew how hard they were both fighting their mutual attraction, though how could she possibly have left him to sleep in his office when she had a spare room?

Luckily there were two parking spaces just outside her house, so they were able to transfer the boxes quickly without having to carry them halfway down the street. Again, Rhys refused to let Katrina lift anything heavy, so she busied herself sorting out a visitor's parking permit for him.

'Is that the last?' she asked, when he brought another box in and stacked it in the hallway.

'Almost. One more.' To her surprise, he returned with the most gorgeous bouquet of white roses and freesias.

She blinked. 'Those are for me?'

He nodded. 'I picked them up on the way home from work—I wanted to say thanks for coming to my rescue.' He smiled. 'I told the florist you didn't do pink.'

'Rhys, they're absolutely beautiful.' Her eyes filmed with tears. She couldn't remember the last time someone had bought her flowers. Pete had stopped buying her flowers a long, long time before their relationship had finally ended. 'Thank you,' she said, her voice breaking slightly.

'If I'd known they'd make you cry, I would've bought you chocolate instead,' he said, and gently wiped the single tear from her cheek with the pad of his thumb. 'Don't cry, *cariad*.'

'Sorry. I just wasn't expecting…' She swallowed hard. Lord. Having him touch her like that—it would be, oh, so easy just to turn her head slightly, press a kiss into his palm.

She got a grip on herself. Just. 'I'll put these in water, then show you to your room. There should be enough space for some of your boxes there, and we can stack the rest in the dining room— that's probably the best place for your cello, too.'

'I don't want to take over your house,' he said, looking awkward.

'You're not. You're staying here as my guest.'

'Actually, I wanted to talk to you about that,' he said as he followed her upstairs, carrying his cases. 'I want to pay you rent while I'm here.'

'Don't be daft. Besides, it's not as if I've ever let the room or anything.'

'Even so, your bills are going to be higher with me staying here, and I want to contribute. And I'll do my share of the chores and cooking.' As if he guessed what she was about to say next, he added, 'No arguments, because you'd say exactly the same if you were the one staying in my spare room while your place was being fixed.'

She couldn't disagree with that. 'All right. Thank you.'

'Good—and I'm going to start by ordering that pizza for us tonight.'

'The number for the best local take-away is by the phone in the kitchen,' she said, showing him into the little guest room. 'And if you want to let your parents or whoever know that you're staying here, feel free to give them my landline.'

'No need. I have a mobile,' he said. 'But thank you for the offer.'

Katrina couldn't quite catch his tone, but she noted the set of his shoulders. It looked as if Rhys's 'don't let anyone close' attitude included his parents. She remembered he'd said his parents had split up; she could understand him being slightly more reserved with the parent who'd left, but surely he would've been close to the one he'd lived with?

Obviously not.

By the time Rhys had unpacked, the pizza had arrived. Katrina was careful not to talk about anything personal, and he seemed to relax again while they ate.

'So do you play your cello very much?' she asked.

'About half an hour a day, to keep in

practice—sometimes more, if it's been a rough day,' he said.

Clearly it was how he unwound at the end of a day. Like the way she lost herself in a book. 'Would you play for me tonight, or are you too tired?'

He looked at her in surprise. 'You'd like me to play for you?'

'As I said earlier, I probably won't appreciate it as much as I should do, but…' She wrinkled her nose. 'I suppose I'm curious. I'd like to know what kind of music you enjoy.'

'Sure. I'll play in your dining room, if you don't mind—it has a wooden floor, so the acoustics will be better,' he said.

'Do you need your sheet music and a stand?'

He shook his head. 'Only if it's something I haven't played for a long while. Most of the pieces I've played for so many years now I know them by heart.'

Katrina watched, fascinated, as Rhys moved a chair into position, removed the cello from its case and tightened the bow.

'I love this one,' he told her. 'It's the second movement of Bach's cello concerto in G minor.'

He really lost himself as he played, she

thought, leaning into the instrument as he moved the bow across the strings. The fingers she'd seen gently treating a child on the ward were just as precise as he pressed each note. And when she looked at his face, it was as if the wall he usually kept between himself and other people had just crumbled away. She was seeing Rhys at his most open—and it brought a lump to her throat. Made her want him even more.

He finished playing and looked up at her.

'Very nice,' she said politely.

'But you had to concentrate.'

She stared at him in surprise. 'How do you know?'

'Because of the pitch being so low. I wondered if you'd be able to hear it properly or if it'd be in your difficult zone.' He looked thoughtful. 'Can I ask you something weird?'

'Weird?'

'Come and sit by me and put your hand against the cello's body, just here.' He touched the lower left side of the cello. 'If you can feel the vibrations, it'll help you hear the music.'

'But won't I get in the way of your bow?'

'No, because my arm will be above your head and the bow's going down to the left.'

'And it won't, um, damage the polish or anything? You know, with the natural oils on my fingertips and what have you?'

He laughed. 'It's not a Stradivarius or a museum piece, Katrina. Just a cello. Touching it won't hurt it at all. Come and sit with me.'

She took a cushion from the sofa, then came to sit at his feet, resting her hand against the cello as he'd directed.

'This is probably my favourite piece by Bach.' He began to play again, and she discovered he was right about the instrument. Feeling the vibration of the note helped her to hear it.

'That's lovely,' she said when he'd finished. 'And I know what that was—the Air on the G String. Dad's got a version of it.'

He nodded.

'Don't stop playing,' she said softly.

The next piece was so beautiful she found herself almost in tears. 'That's amazing. What is it?'

'The *adagio cantabile* from Beethoven's Pathétique Sonata. Strictly speaking, it's a piano piece—but I think it works on the cello, too.' He shrugged. 'I used to drive my cello teacher crazy, transcribing my favourite piano pieces.'

'But you play so well. I think I'm beginning to understand why Maddie loves music so much.'

'Music's food for the soul,' he said softly.

'Would it be greedy to ask for more?'

'You want more, young Oliver?' he teased.

She took her hand from the cello. 'Sorry.'

'I was teasing.' He switched the bow to his other hand, then reached down with his right hand to take hers. 'If you'd like me to play a bit more, it'd be my pleasure.'

Lord, the touch of his hand against hers… She couldn't help curling her fingers round his. For a long, long moment they said nothing, just looked at each other. And Katrina found herself wondering what it would be like to feel his hands against her skin. Would he touch her with the same precision as he played the notes? Would he coax the same kind of response from her body that he coaxed from the cello?

It was, oh, so tempting.

But there would always be a morning after the night before. And given that they both had issues, she really needed to take a metaphorical step backwards. Right now.

'So Bach's your favourite composer?' she asked brightly, uncurling her fingers.

She saw the acknowledgement in his eyes: that he'd been thinking exactly the same thing. Wondering what it would be like to touch her properly. Wondering how she'd react to his hands, his mouth.

'Definitely. Actually, I ache a bit from lugging boxes around. I'll play you more another time.'

'I'll go and put the kettle on,' Katrina said. And the awkward moment was avoided, she thought.

For now.

CHAPTER SEVEN

THE following morning, when Katrina got up, she could smell coffee. Clearly Rhys was up already. She showered and dressed swiftly, and walked into the kitchen. 'Good morning.'

'Morning,' he replied.

'And you've made coffee. Wonderful.' She smiled. 'I think I could get used to this.'

'Ah, no. It'll be your turn to make the coffee tomorrow,' he said lightly.

'Did you sleep OK?'

'Very well, thanks.'

'Good.' She rummaged in the cupboard. 'Cereals or toast?'

'You don't have to make breakfast for me or wait on me, Katrina.'

'I know. But I'm making toast for myself, and it's as quick to stick four slices of bread under the grill as it is two,' she pointed out.

'Then toast would be lovely. Thanks.' He poured them both a mug of coffee, adding milk to hers. 'Well. Cheers.'

'Cheers.'

It had been a long time since Katrina had shared her space like this. But she actually found herself enjoying it—and it would be was good to have company on the walk to work.

After breakfast, she enjoyed walking in to work with Rhys; in the weeks since Madison had moved, Katrina had missed walking in to the hospital with her cousin.

Sharing a house somehow made them more in tune at work, too. 'Can I borrow you for a minute?' Katrina asked one afternoon, leaning against the doorjamb to Rhys's office.

'Sure. What's the problem?'

'Little girl, four years old, history of UTIs. No history in her siblings, but I'm wondering if there's an underlying problem.'

'Are you thinking VUR?' he asked.

VUR, or vesico-ureteric reflux, was when the valve between the bladder and the tubes that led from the kidneys to the bladder didn't work properly, allowing urine to flow back towards the kidneys.

'It's only a suspicion. I haven't done any tests yet.'

'Start with an ultrasound,' he said, 'though it's very easy to miss any signs of scarring, depending on what grade of VUR you're looking at and whether your patient has a fever. You might have to do a cystogram.'

'I hope not,' she said. 'It's unpleasant for little ones, even if you do some play therapy with them first to prepare them for the procedure.' The cystogram meant putting a catheter in the little girl's urethra and filling her bladder with a liquid that showed up on X-ray, then doing a scan to see if all the liquid was going through the urethra or if any was going back towards the kidneys.

'Want me to come and have a look?' he asked.

'Please.'

Katrina introduced him to her patient, Annabel, and her mother, and Rhys explained what they suspected.

'We're going to take a magic picture of your tummy,' Katrina said to Annabel. 'It won't hurt, but it might tickle a bit because I have to put some special gel on your tummy to help me take the picture.' She showed the scanning head to the little girl and let her hold it so she wasn't scared, then swiftly did the scan.

Rhys looked at the screen. 'There's definitely some scarring there,' he said.

'So the good news is that we don't have to do any further tests that Annabel might find uncomfortable,' Katrina explained to Annabel's mother.

'And even better news is that although it's vesico-ureteric reflux, I can't see any distension. We grade the condition from one to five, with one being the mildest,' he said, 'and this looks like a grade two to me. So it should clear up on its own without surgery.'

'What causes it?' Annabel's mother asked.

'With small children, it's usually caused by the tunnel through the bladder wall not being long enough,' Rhys said.

'As she grows, the tunnel will get longer and the condition will improve,' Katrina added. 'But we need to make sure Annabel doesn't get any more urine infections, or it might cause some damage to her kidneys.'

'And to make sure she doesn't get an infection, we'll give her long-term antibiotic therapy—a very low dose every day until she's five,' Rhys said.

'But doesn't using antibiotics lead to bugs becoming resistant?' Annabel's mother asked.

'If you don't complete the course properly, yes. But this is slightly different,' Katrina said. 'She'll need to give regular urine samples to your GP, and we'll call her in for an ultrasound every six months to check that her kidneys are growing properly. And if you get any signs of a urinary infection, you need to take her straight to your doctor.'

'So that's if she starts needing to have a wee more often than usual or has accidents that just aren't like her,' Rhys said. 'Or if she's not very well and you can't put your finger on what's wrong, she gets a temperature, or her urine smells unpleasant or has blood in it.'

'Will giving her cranberry juice help?' Annabel's mother asked.

'Should do, but look out for the other signs as well,' Katrina advised.

'So she'll definitely grow out of it?'

'I'm pretty sure she will,' Rhys said. 'If not, we'll need to give her an operation to correct the valve problem—but try not to worry. In most cases the antibiotic treatment works really well and it's more than likely she'll outgrow the condition.'

'We'll need to scan her big brother and her little sister, just to check they're not affected,' Katrina added.

'Because about a third of patients with VUR also have siblings with the condition,' Rhys explained.

'I can book them in for the scans now, if you like,' Katrina said.

'Thank you.' Annabel's mother smiled. 'You've worked together for a long time, haven't you?'

'A little while,' Rhys said.

'I thought so.'

'Why?' he asked.

'Because you finish each other's sentences.'

'Do we?' Katrina blinked. 'I hadn't—'

'Noticed,' Rhys continued with a grin. 'It's called teamwork.'

'Everyone on the ward does it,' Katrina said. Though even as she spoke, she wondered. Did they? Or were she and Rhys just that little bit more in tune?

She was still wondering on the Saturday morning, in a world of her own, when she walked into the bathroom, shrugged off her robe, pulled the shower curtain back from the edge of the bath—and saw Rhys there, showering off the last suds.

'Oh, my God. I'm so sorry. I didn't realise…I didn't hear…I'm *so* sorry.' She felt colour shoot into her face; mortified, she grabbed her robe and fled from the room.

It felt as if everything was happening in slow motion. The curtain being dragged back, the look of shock on Katrina's face as she saw him, followed swiftly by embarrassment, and then she rushed away.

Clearly he hadn't locked the door properly and she hadn't heard the water running. And the last thing Rhys wanted was for Katrina to feel embarrassed about her hearing or be awkward with him because of it. He turned off the shower with one hand and grabbed a towel and wrapped it round himself with the other as he climbed out of the bathtub. Heedless of the fact he was still wet, he went after her, catching up with her in the corridor by her bedroom door. 'Katrina, wait.' He put a hand on her arm to get her attention and make her face him.

'I'm sorry,' she said again, biting her lip. She looked embarrassed and close to tears, and he hated it. He couldn't let her shut herself away in her room, feeling that upset and miserable.

'It's all right,' he said, making sure that she could see his face. 'It's my fault—I couldn't have locked the bathroom door properly. You didn't hear the water running?'

'No. I wasn't concentrating.' She gulped. 'I'm so sorry.'

'*Cariad*, please don't keep apologising. It isn't your fault. You weren't expecting me to be there and I should have made sure the door was locked so you knew I was there.' He stroked her face. 'I'm sorry—you said you weren't profoundly deaf, and I didn't realise quite how much hearing loss you have.'

'It's the family joke that I'm always the one who sleeps through thunderstorms.' She gave him a brittle smile. 'It's just as well I'm a lark instead of an owl like Maddie, or I'd never hear the alarm and be up in time for work. Mum bought me one of those ones that uses a light instead of sound and gradually gets brighter like the sun, and Dad made sure my smoke detectors are really loud so I'm safe, and Maddie bought me one of those gizmos that flashes when the phone or doorbell rings.'

She was gabbling, and they both knew it.

'Maybe you should sing in the shower in future or something,' she said. 'Very, very loudly.'

Katrina was clearly trying to make light of the situation, but Rhys heard the slight crack in her voice. She was really upset. And embarrassed. And feeling she was lacking in something. No doubt she was thinking about Pete and his cruel, unfair comments.

'Katrina, never, *ever* apologise for being you. You're fine just the way you are.' Even though he knew it was dangerous and he really shouldn't do it—he wanted to comfort her and make her feel better. Which meant putting his arms round her, holding her close.

She was wearing a soft white towelling dressing-gown; when he pressed his cheek against hers, her skin felt even softer.

Irresistible.

He couldn't stop himself. He turned his face very, very slightly until the corner of his mouth was touching hers. The lightest, sweetest, gentlest kiss. And then everything seemed to blur. He wasn't quite sure when or how it happened, but then Katrina was holding him back, her arms wrapped just as tightly round him as his were round her, and her mouth was against his properly. Warm and sweet and soft and responsive, opening under the pressure of his mouth so he could deepen the kiss.

He could feel the blood pulsing through his veins. Feel his heart beating, strong and quickening as he kissed her. Feel every sense magnifying, blooming.

This was exactly what he'd thought it would be like, kissing Katrina.

Amazing.

Even though part of him told him to stop, that he was in grave danger of making the situation much worse, his need for her was stronger. He couldn't remember ever wanting anyone so much. And it was as if a dam had broken, the feeling rushing through him, powerful and unstoppable.

She'd put her bathrobe back on but he knew she was naked underneath. In that brief moment when she'd slipped off her robe in the bathroom, he'd seen just how lovely she was. And he needed to see her again. To touch her. To taste her. He needed that so very, very badly. Still kissing her, he undid the belt of her robe in one fluid movement and pushed the fabric off her shoulders—and then he broke the kiss. Brushed his mouth against hers, just to tell her he had every intention of kissing her again. And then he stepped back far enough to look at her properly.

Lord, she was gorgeous.

He stroked his palms over her shoulders and down her arms, gliding his hands upwards again over her hips and settling in the curve of her waist.

He made a small sound of pure pleasure. '*Cariad*, you're so beautiful. You take my breath away.'

She said nothing, just looked at him, her blue eyes huge and full of wonder and fear; and Rhys knew in that moment that she felt exactly the same as he did. Wanting this so much, but scared in case everything went wrong and crashed down around them.

Maybe it was time to be brave.

He dipped his head and traced a line of kisses round her throat. Her skin was so soft, so sweet. And he wanted more.

As she tipped her head back, he let his mouth drift lower, then took one nipple into his mouth.

She breathed a little, 'Oh' and slid her fingers

into his hair. The gentle pressure of her fingertips against his scalp urged him on, telling him she liked what he was doing; he switched his attention to her other nipple, teasing it with his tongue and his lips until she was pushing against him, clearly wanting more.

'You're gorgeous,' he said huskily, stroking over her ribcage to the flat planes of her stomach. Her breathing was fast and shallow, much like his own. 'And I want you, Katrina. I need...' He straightened up again so he could look her in the eye. 'I think we *both* need this.'

'Yes,' she whispered. She opened her door and walked through it, leaving her towelling robe where it lay on the floor in the hallway.

The soft light filtered through her bedroom curtains and he could see her very clearly. 'You're amazing, Katrina,' he said, following her and closing the door behind him. 'Stunning.'

She actually blushed.

Did she really not know how lovely she was?

And then she smiled and he lost his head completely. He pulled her back into his arms and kissed her again, stroking her back and the curve of her buttocks. She felt perfect. 'I want to touch you, Katrina. I want to touch you all over,' he said between kisses. He wanted to learn what she liked, what gave her pleasure, to make her feel as amazing as she made him feel.

Almost shyly, she tugged at the edge of his towel. It fell to the floor—and then at last there was nothing between them. Skin to damp skin. And it felt so very, very good.

He wasn't quite sure how they got there or who led whom, but then they were lying facing each other in her bed, the cotton sheet cool against their bodies. Right at that moment he felt as if he was burning up with need for her. He let the flat of his hand slide over her curves, moulding itself to the dip of her waist and the swell of her hip.

'Perfect,' he breathed. Then he remembered: she wouldn't hear what he was saying. He shifted so she could read his lips, and repeated, 'You're absolutely perfect.' His fingers trailed along her outer thigh, then gently brushed upwards again, this time against her inner thigh. Katrina shivered and moved slightly, allowing him the access he craved so badly. He cupped her sex, then let one finger glide along the soft, sweet folds.

She gasped as his fingertip skated across her clitoris.

'You like that?' he asked.

'Yes.'

He did it again.

'Oh-h-h.' The word was a breath of pure pleasure.

He bent to kiss her, still stroking her and teasing her until she was making little incoherent noises.

And then a truly awful thought struck him.

'Katrina.' He touched her shoulder to get her attention.

'Hmm?' She opened her eyes, blinking to help her focus. 'What?'

'Do you have any condoms?'

'Condoms?' she echoed. Her eyes widened; clearly she realised exactly what his question implied. 'No.'

'Ah.'

'Are you telling me you don't either?'

'I don't either,' he said ruefully.

'And I'm not on the Pill.' She took a deep breath.

But there was a slight wobble in her voice, telling him that she was as disappointed as he was. That he'd brought her to this pitch of arousal and now he was going to let her down.

Well, he wasn't going to let her down.

'There's another way,' he said softly, and leaned over to kiss her, sliding one hand back between her thighs.

'Rhys…'

'Shh. It's OK,' he soothed, and kissed his way down her body, nuzzling all the way down her sternum, drawing a line of teasing kisses around her navel and finally stroking her thighs apart.

He drew one finger along the length of her sex, and she quivered.

He did it again and again, taking it slowly, feeling the heat build between them.

When he pushed one finger inside her, she gave a gasp of pleasure. 'Yes,' she whispered. 'Oh, Rhys—please, yes.'

He circled her clitoris with his thumb as he moved his hand, gradually quickening his pace, kissing her deeply until he felt her go rigid.

'Open your eyes, *cariad*,' he said, stroking her cheek with the back of his fingers.

She did. And it gave him such a kick to see the

wonder in her eyes, the sheer pleasure, followed by the soft, sweet aftershocks of her climax rippling over his skin.

'Oh. My. God,' Katrina said, her voice shaky. Her pupils, he was pleased to note, were absolutely huge. 'Rhys, that was… I mean…'

He loved it that he'd been able to reduce this clever, capable woman to incoherent mush. That he'd made her feel so good she lost it completely.

'Good,' he said, and stole another kiss.

She dragged in a breath. 'My turn.'

'You don't have to.' He moved so that he was lying on his side. 'That's not the way it works, *cariad.*'

'But I…Rhys, you made me feel amazing just now.'

'Good. That was the point. Because you *are* amazing, Katrina.'

'And I should do the same for—'

He silenced her with a kiss. 'There's no shoulds in this.' He couldn't resist kissing her again. 'That wasn't actually supposed to happen. It certainly wasn't planned. I just couldn't keep my hands off you. Once I'd touched you, kissed you—I couldn't stop.'

'So what now?'

That was the big question. And trust her to face it head-on rather than skirt round the issue. 'I like you, Katrina. A lot. And I feel different when I'm with you.'

'But?' She said the word for him.

'But I don't know if I can offer you what you deserve.' He grimaced. 'I'm not good at relationships. I start out with good intentions and then somehow there's this glass wall between me and the woman I'm falling for, and it all goes horribly wrong. I don't want to do that to you—especially after what happened with Pete. I don't want to hurt you.' Even though he knew he really ought to resume the distance between them, try and go back to how things had been before, he needed her back in his arms. He wrapped his arms round her and shifted so that she was lying with her head resting on his shoulder and her arm wrapped round his waist. 'But we've crossed a line here. I don't think we can go back to how it was. Not now I know how it feels to touch you.'

'Me, too,' she admitted. 'And I want to make you feel the way you just made *me* feel. Incredible.'

'You don't have to.'

'I want to.' She stroked his hip. 'I want to touch you, Rhys. I want to make you lose it, the way you made me lose it just now. I want to blow your mind.'

'Carry on like this, *cariad*, and I'm going to forget all about being sensible,' he warned her softly.

She removed her hand. 'Sorry.'

'Don't be.' He stole another kiss. 'We discussed it. We agreed to stay apart. And it didn't work.' He paused. 'So let's try it the other way.'

'You mean—be lovers?'

'Yes. I want to be your lover,' he said, drawing the pad of his thumb along her lower lip. 'I want to take you to the very edge of pleasure.' He wanted to lose himself within her and forget the world.

'Lovers.' She shivered slightly as she said the word, but he knew she wasn't cold. Very, very far from it. The thought clearly excited her as much as it excited him. Her pupils were huge and her lips were parted and it was all he could do not to kiss her again.

She dragged in a breath. 'This scares the hell out of me, Rhys.'

'Me, too,' he admitted. 'But maybe it's time we were both brave. See where this takes us.'

'But keep it just between us for now,' Katrina said.

While this was all so new. He knew exactly where she was coming from. 'Yes.' He kissed her lightly. Just to seal the deal. 'If I stay here with you any longer, Katrina, I'm going to do something reckless.' He kissed her again. 'So I suggest we get up. I'm going to finish that shower. I'd prefer it to be with you wrapped round me, but I'm going to show restraint and shower on my own—because I'm rapidly running out of willpower where you're concerned.'

'Uh-huh.'

'And that wasn't the first brick going up in the glass wall,' he reassured her, seeing the sudden worry in her expression. 'Because, after you've had a shower, we're going out. I don't mind where we go or what we do, but I'm going to make a very necessary purchase at some point today. And then I plan to take you out to dinner. And tonight, Katrina Gregory, I'm going to make love with you properly. The way I've wanted to since practically the first moment I met you.'

She looked at him, half-shy and so achingly sweet he very nearly forgot himself and made love with her anyway. 'I sincerely hope that's a promise,' she said.

He smiled. 'Oh, it is. And, Katrina?'

'Mmm?'

'Just so you know…I always…' he kissed her, just for emphasis '…*always* keep my promises.'

CHAPTER EIGHT

AFTER his shower, Rhys dressed, headed for the kitchen and made a cafetière of coffee. He was sitting flicking through a medical journal, nursing a mug of coffee, when Katrina strolled into the room. Dressed casually in jeans and a light sweater, she looked absolutely edible; and when she gave him a shy, sweet smile, he really had to stop himself scooping her up, settling her on his lap and drinking the rest of his coffee with one arm wrapped round her.

Instead, he put the journal on the table and wrapped his hands round his coffee mug to keep them occupied. 'Hi. Coffee's still hot if you want some.'

'This is getting to be a habit, you making me coffee.' She smiled. 'But it's one I could get used to.' She poured herself a mugful, adding plenty of milk. 'Have you had breakfast yet?'

'I waited for you.'

She smiled. 'Then humour me. I'm going to experiment.'

'Experiment?' Oh, the thoughts that word conjured up.

She flushed to the roots of her hair, and he smiled. 'You're delicious. And I like the fact that your mind works the same way as mine.'

'Stop it. I'm going to make breakfast. Get on with reading your journal.'

Was she trying to keep her hands occupied, he wondered, just like he was, so they didn't end up ripping off each other's clothes again?

And then he wished he hadn't thought of that. Because he really, really wanted to take Katrina back to bed and spend the day discovering just where she liked to be touched, where she liked to be kissed.

She busied herself whipping up something in a bowl and heating butter in an omelette pan.

Pancakes for breakfast? he guessed. Sounded good to him.   'I'll get plates and cutlery,' he said. Mainly because it meant he had to walk right past her and that gave him the perfect opportunity to drop a kiss on the nape of her neck.

Just so she knew he hadn't changed his mind while she'd been in the shower. That he still wanted her.

And then, when she tipped the contents of the bowl onto a board, rolled it out and cut out rounds, he realised what she'd just made.

Dough for Welsh cakes.

Not quite traditional ones, as she hadn't added sultanas. But he could smell the sweet scent of cinnamon. And something else.

'These are gorgeous,' he said after the first bite. 'Cinnamon?'

'Sorry, it's not quite traditional—but I loathe sultanas,' Katrina said. 'And the vanilla's my mum's trick.' She smiled. 'I love the scent of vanilla. And you can't beat a really good vanilla ice cream.'

Eaten in bed, he thought, from one of the small half-litre tubs, sharing the spoon and feeding each other and…

'Rhys?'

He shook himself mentally. 'Sorry. Just thinking.' But the picture was still there in his mind, and he couldn't help the words sliding out. 'You. Ice cream. Bed.'

She dragged in a breath. *'Rhys.'*

Her expression mirrored the longing in his head. Clearly she could imagine it, too.

'We can't.' Lord, it was hard to call a halt when his whole body was crying out to him to just pick her up, carry her to her bed and make love with her until they were both out of their minds. 'We need…'

'Supplies,' she finished.

'Waiting's going to make it even better,' he said. Though right at that moment he wasn't sure he believed that. Every sweet-scented bite of the Welsh cakes made him think of the sweetness of Katrina's mouth and how much he wanted to kiss her.

Katrina had just about managed to get her libido back under control by the time they'd finished washing up. Though the look in Rhys's eyes made breathing difficult. It made her remember just how it had felt when he'd kissed her, touched her, stroked her until her body had surged into a climax.

He'd expected nothing in return. Even turned down her offer to reciprocate.

Later tonight, she promised herself, she'd make it up to him.

And how.

She dragged on her fleece while he shrugged on a battered leather jacket. Added to his worn jeans and black sweater, it made him look dangerous. Sexy as hell. Katrina actually had to remind herself to breathe.

He held her hand all the way to the tube station. All the way on the tube. And all the way while they walked on Hampstead Heath, kicking through piles of autumn leaves.

'I've missed this,' he said, looking wistful.

'So Cardiff is full of trees and parks?'

'Not quite in the same way as London,' he said. 'I was thinking more of the village where I grew up. There's a ruined castle with a huge park. I had a holiday job in the tearooms. And, best of all, it meant I got free entrance, so on a dry day I could study under the shade of a tree in the park. Just me, my books and the fresh air.' He smiled. 'And I used to really love walking there in the autumn. Crunching through the leaves and collecting the odd conker.'

Why hadn't he studied at home in comfort,

like she and Madison had? Katrina wondered. And if Rhys loved the countryside that much, it seemed odd that he'd chosen to work in a city hospital, rather than as a country GP where he'd get a chance to do house calls and be outside a lot. Or maybe it was something to do with the difficult family life he'd mentioned. A place of escape.

They had lunch, a panini and coffee, in a small café, then spent the rest of the afternoon browsing in the antique and bric-a-brac shops. When he spotted a chemist's shop, Rhys excused himself, and Katrina felt her face heat. She knew exactly what he was going to buy. And she knew that getting 'supplies' was the right thing to do—but she also knew that she was going to spend the rest of the afternoon thinking about what they would do that evening when they got home.

Making love.

The ultimate in closeness.

The weight of his body over hers.

His body moving inside hers.

Excitement and desire shimmered down her spine.

When he walked back out into the street, she couldn't think straight. And clearly she had some kind of goofy look on her face, because he asked softly, 'Are you all right, Katrina?'

'I'm fine,' she fibbed.

'Good.' He took her hand, drew it up to his mouth and kissed the backs of her fingers. 'I think,' he said softly, 'we should have an early dinner.'

She felt her eyes widen. 'Rhys, we're not really dressed...'

'For an expensive restaurant, no.' He drew her close to him and bent his head so he could whisper in her ear. 'Katrina.'

She loved it that he'd thought to check she could hear him. 'Yes?'

'I would love to see you all dressed up. Especially knowing that I'd have the privilege later of undressing you again.'

His words sent a lovely shivery feeling all the way through her.

'But the thing is, if we go back now and change, we might not get past the stage of taking *these* clothes off.'

Oh, lord. The pictures that put in her head.

His mouth brushed the sensitive spot by her

ear. 'So let's go somewhere a little more casual. Eat. And then I'm taking you home.'

In the end they found a small trattoria. With candles and flowers on the table, the place felt incredibly romantic. Especially as their table was in a quiet corner, Katrina thought.

Every time she caught Rhys's eye, every time her fingers brushed against his when they dipped their bread in the little dish of olive oil, a little throb of excitement pulsed through her. She could see on his face that it was the same for him. And when the waiter brought the dessert menu to them and asked them if they wanted coffee, Rhys glanced at her. She gave the tiniest shake of her head. She didn't want pudding or coffee. Just him.

'Just the bill, please,' Rhys said with a smile.

Every second they waited seemed to take for ever. Every step back to the tube felt like a mile. And the wait on the platform for a train, watching the clock and willing the minutes to speed by instead of drag by...

'It's a pity the train's so empty,' Rhys said when it finally arrived.

'Why?' she asked, mystified.

'Because if it was full you'd have had to... Ah,

what the hell. We'll do it anyway.' He sat down and pulled her onto his lap, catching her off balance so she had to put her arms round his neck for support.

'Now, that,' he said with a smile, 'feels better.'

They didn't talk on the train. Didn't need to. And Rhys held her hand all the way from the tube station to her house. With every step, Katrina's heart was racing. And the second the front door closed behind them, he spun her into his arms, dipped his head and kissed her.

She felt him slip her fleecy jacket off and drop it on the floor. His leather jacket followed.

'Leave them,' he said softly. 'I'll deal with it later. We've been sensible all day and I just can't wait any more. I want you so much, Katrina.' He took her hand again. Held her gaze. Kissed the tip of each finger, drawing it briefly into his mouth. She could see the flare of desire brighten in his eyes. And then he laced his fingers through hers.

'I could do the caveman thing.'

'You could,' she agreed neutrally.

'But I need to be sure you want this as much as I do. That I'm not pushing you.'

In answer, she drew his hands up to her

mouth and kissed them. 'You're not pushing me. And I do want this. And I'm quite happy to be carried off by a gorgeous Welsh knight, even if his white charger isn't actually with him.' She stroked his face. 'Except I'm not little, like Maddie, so I don't want you to do your back in.'

He laughed. 'Ah, now, *cariad*, you're impugning my masculinity.'

She smiled and pressed herself against him. 'I'm well aware that you're a man, Rhys.' All man. And how.

He dragged in a breath. 'And you are irresistible, Katrina Gregory. Not girly—but you're definitely all woman.' He cupped her face, holding her very tenderly, as if she were something infinitely precious. He dipped his head, brushing his mouth against hers in a sweet, gentle kiss. And the second their lips touched, the kiss turned explosive, his tongue sliding against hers and mimicking the way his body would fill her later. Promising and demanding, at the same time. Cherishing and possessive. Claiming her as his and yet making it clear that what they were about to do would be very, very mutual.

She'd never wanted anyone as much as she wanted Rhys Morgan.

And when he finally broke the kiss, ending with a sweet, gentle caress and pulling back enough to look her in the eye, she whispered, 'Now.'

She laced her fingers through his and led him up the stairs.

At the top, he paused. 'And this is where I carry you to my room.'

Katrina shook her head. 'My bed's a double. Yours is a single and I'm too old to behave like a student.'

'Old? Twenty-eight is hardly old.' But he humoured her, let her draw him down the corridor to her room. At her doorway, he paused again. 'Katrina.'

'Yes?'

'Caveman or knight. It's the same thing.' He pushed her door open, scooped her up and carried her over the threshold. He set her on her feet next to the bed, drew the curtains, then took the hem of her sweater and drew it upwards. She lifted her arms, letting him pull off her sweater; he traced along the lacy edges of her bra with one fingertip, a look of wonder on his face, clearly enjoying the contrast between the stiffness of the lace and the softness of her skin.

'You're so beautiful, *cariad*.'

She felt her face heat, and tried to cover her confusion by saying, 'And you're wearing way too much.'

'Want to do something about it?'

She nodded, and he let her strip off his sweater. She stroked his arms, his shoulders, glorying in the feel of his skin under her fingertips, then let her hands trail down over his chest to his abdomen. 'Rhys Morgan, you're beautiful, too.' She couldn't remember desiring anyone so much. Rhys was just perfect. He wasn't lean and skinny, but he wasn't fat either—just beautifully toned, with powerful shoulders and strong biceps and narrow hips and strong thighs. He really did look like the Welsh knight she'd teased about being— noble, beautiful, his dark hair in sharp contrast to his pale skin and blue eyes. Perfect Celtic colouring. She could just imagine him as a knight, hundreds of years ago, his hair slightly longer. Sexy as hell.

'*Cariad?* What are you thinking?' he asked.

She told him, and he grinned. 'Now, as the

knight I'd have the honour of bedding my maiden fair.' His expression sobered. 'And that's exactly what I want to do with you right now, Katrina.'

He drew one finger along her breastbone, then with his other hand he unsnapped her bra and let it fall to the floor. When he cupped her breasts, she tipped her head back, baring her throat to him. He took full advantage, kissing his way down her throat and stooping lower so he could take one nipple into his mouth. She dragged in a breath as he teased the hard peak with the tip of his tongue and then sucked hard. 'Rhys.'

He stopped immediately. 'You don't like this?'

'Ye-es.'

'But?'

She swallowed hard. 'It's not *enough*. I need you, Rhys. Now. All day I've been thinking about you. About us. About tonight. And if you don't make love with me this very second, I think I'm going to spontaneously combust.'

'Your wish,' he said, 'is my command.' He undid the button of her jeans, slid the zip down, and gently pushed the soft denim over her hips. She shimmied out of her jeans and kicked off her socks at the same time, so she was standing before him in nothing but a tiny pair of white lace knickers.

She was pleased to note that his pupils dilated and colour bloomed in his cheeks. 'Katrina. I…' He shook his head, as if clearing it, then stripped off the rest of his clothes in three seconds flat, picked her up and laid her on the bed.

His hands were sure yet gentle as he tipped her back against the pillows, and when he kissed his way down her body, she could feel the faint rasp of stubble. And somehow he found erogenous zones she hadn't even known existed, making her wriggle beneath him, desperate for more. He circled her navel with his tongue, nuzzled her hipbones, and finally, finally slid his hands between her thighs, parting them. But when his hands moved lower, caressing the backs of her knees, she almost whimpered.

'Rhys. Stop teasing me. Please. I need…'

'I know. So do I. Hold that thought,' he whispered, and stole a kiss before climbing off the bed.

Despite being completely naked, he was totally unselfconscious; Katrina couldn't help watching him as he moved. He really was beautiful. Perfect musculature beneath that smooth skin. And she *wanted*. Lord, how she wanted.

He rummaged in his jeans, took the packet of condoms he'd bought earlier from the pocket and removed one.

'My job, I think,' she said, taking it from him as he joined her on the bed again. She undid the foil packet, then slid the condom over his erect penis, and she was gratified when he gave a sharp intake of breath. So he was in the same state as she was? Good.

He knelt between her thighs, and she sank back against the pillows. Just as she'd done that morning, when he'd tipped her over the edge of pleasure, unselfishly making sure that she was sated even though he hadn't been.

And now...

Rhys kissed her again, then whispered, 'Katrina?'

She opened her eyes. 'Yes?'

'Now?'

'Now,' she confirmed.

Slowly, gently, he eased his body into hers.

Katrina had had sex before. Made love before.

But nothing had been like this. The way Rhys made her feel…

'This feels like paradise,' Rhys said softly.

That pretty much summed it up for her, too.

He slid his hands up her thighs, gently positioning her so that her legs were wrapped round his waist, and then he pushed deeper. Katrina couldn't help giving a little 'oh' of pleasure. Rhys smiled, but not as if he was smugly pleased with himself—more that he was pleased he was making her feel so good.

He kissed her throat—hot, wet, open-mouthed kisses that had her quivering and clutching at his shoulders, wanting him even closer, needing the ultimate contact. She was aware of the hardness of his chest against the softness of her breasts, and the friction of the hair against her sensitised nipples was driving her crazy.

And then, as if Rhys knew she was right near the edge, he slowed everything down. Slowly, incredibly focused, he withdrew until he was almost out of her, then slid all the way back in again, putting pressure on just the right spot and making her feel as if she were floating.

When her climax hit, it felt like being in the

middle of a storm, the dark skies lit by sheets of lightning.

'Now,' he whispered, and jammed his mouth against hers; she felt his body surge against hers, and knew that he too had just fallen over the edge.

Afterwards, she lay curled in his arms. 'Any regrets?' he asked softly.

'No.'

'Good.'

Part of her was almost too scared to ask, but she needed to know. 'You?'

He stroked her face. 'No.'

'Good.'

'But?'

It amazed her that he could read her so easily. That he'd picked up on the tiny, tiny fear. 'I was just wondering…were you planning to go back to your own room?'

'If you want me to.' He shifted so he could look her in the eye. 'But if there's a choice of sleeping with you in my arms and waking up with you tomorrow morning…I'd definitely pick that one.'

Exactly what she wanted, too. 'Yes,' she said softly.

While he was in the bathroom, dealing with the condom, she removed her hearing aid and placed it in the case that she kept next to the clock. When he returned, he said something she didn't catch.

'Sorry. I'm minus sound,' she said, feeling her face heat. 'I, um, don't sleep with my hearing aid in.'

He kissed the tip of her nose. 'No need to apologise. I asked if you were sure about this.'

'I'm sure.'

'Good.' And, with that, he slid into bed beside her, switched off the light and gathered her into his arms, holding her close.

Katrina felt her eyelids droop; safe and secure in Rhys's arms, she drifted off to sleep.

CHAPTER NINE

KATRINA woke twice in the night. Once when she kissed Rhys awake and, while all his defences were down, repaid him the pleasure he'd given her that morning. And once when she was startled out of a bad dream, and cuddled into him as if having his arms round her would protect her from the nameless fears that still lingered. As if he sensed it, he tightened his arms and murmured something she didn't catch but which made her feel safe again.

And then it was morning.

Sunday morning, when neither of them had to be at the hospital.

When she woke, she half expected Rhys to be up already, reading the paper or a magazine at the kitchen table and nursing a cup of coffee, but he was still curled around her, holding her close.

It felt very, very odd.

She wasn't used to waking up in someone's arms. Not since Pete.

And today was a whole new day. Despite what they'd shared the previous night, would it be different now between them? Would Rhys have had time to think about it and come to the same conclusions that Pete had? Would he back away?

She stretched, very slightly, and was rewarded with a kiss in the curve between her neck and shoulder.

Oh.

So he was awake.

How long had he been awake? Had she snored or embarrassed herself by talking in her sleep or anything? The fears flurried through her mind.

'Good morning, sleepyhead.' His voice was clear, slightly amused. 'I thought you said you were a lark?'

'I am.' It couldn't be much past seven.

Then she glanced at the clock. 'Nine o'clock?' she asked in horror. 'But I never sleep in this late!' She twisted round to face him.

'Neither do I. But I didn't want to move,' he admitted. 'I liked waking up with you in my arms, all soft and warm.'

So he hadn't changed his mind. He'd been awake for ages and he'd just wanted to hold her.

Warmth spread through her and her worries faded away. Maybe, just maybe, she thought, this was going to work out just fine.

'So what now?' she asked.

'I thought we could take a shower. A long one. Together. And it's miserable weather outside, so I'll make us some breakfast. If there's something on at the cinema, maybe we could go out.' He stroked her face. 'And if there's not… Well, I'll just have to lie with you on the sofa and watch a film here.'

A lazy Sunday afternoon in autumn spent with Rhys. She couldn't think of anything she'd rather do. 'Sounds good to me.'

The shower took a long, long time, and Katrina knew afterwards that she'd never be able to see her bathroom in quite the same light again. She'd always remember the way Rhys had lifted her against the tiles, the way the water had poured over their bodies as her body had tightened round his, the way he'd soaped her all over afterwards and dried her in a warm, fluffy towel.

Breakfast was forgotten; it was more like lunchtime when they finally made it downstairs. When they checked the cinema listings, there wasn't anything on that either of them was keen to see. Glancing out of the window at the kind of drizzle she knew from experience was miserably penetrating, Katrina didn't really want to go out anyway. They ended up cooking Sunday lunch together and having a quiet, domesticated day indoors— one of the sweetest, loveliest days Katrina had ever spent. They closed the curtains against the rain to watch a *film noir*, curled up together on the sofa, and afterwards Rhys played the cello for her before making love with her again.

If she'd been able to stop time and bottle it, she thought, she would've chosen that day. Because it was just perfect.

The next few weeks were the happiest Katrina had ever known. At work they kept things strictly professional, only having lunch together if it was a case conference on a patient, but outside she spent nearly all her free time with him.

Madison was right, Katrina thought. She *had* been missing out. And she knew without a doubt that Rhys was The One.

He hadn't actually told her he loved her. Just

as she hadn't told him. But she knew. It was in his eyes, in the way he touched her, in the way he surprised her with tickets to a rarely shown film, in the way he made sure she could see his face when he said anything to her.

And even though Rhys moved back into his flat when the landlord had given him the all-clear after the roof repairs, he still spent his nights with her—either at his place or hers. She even kept a toothbrush and spare clothes at his places, as he did at hers.

Life didn't get any better than this, Katrina thought. And he was gradually letting her close. Maybe, just maybe, things were going to work out. For both of them.

'I'm the one who's supposed to be glowing,' Madison remarked, adding far too much pepper to her mushroom and avocado pizza.

'You are glowing.' Then Katrina realised what her cousin meant. 'If you're asking if I'm pregnant, don't be daft. Of course I'm not. Clearly these cravings for disgusting pizza toppings are addling your brain.'

Madison rolled her eyes. 'There's nothing disgusting about avocado on pizza. And I wasn't saying that you were pregnant. Just glowing. As in the glow that means you're having absolutely loads of fantastic sex.'

'Maddie!'

Her cousin grinned, totally unrepentant. 'Well, you are, aren't you?'

Katrina felt herself blushing to the roots of her hair. 'Yes.'

'Excellent. It's good to see you happy, Kat. He's the one, isn't he?'

Katrina had quietly confided to her cousin that she was seeing Rhys. 'We're taking it day by day.'

'But you're in love with him, aren't you?'

'I'm not saying the words.'

Madison raised an eyebrow. 'Take the risk. It's worth it, I promise you.'

'Not yet.' There was still something holding Katrina back. She wasn't sure what, but she couldn't say it just yet. It was too new. And she'd only recently realised herself just how deeply her feelings went for Rhys. It was as if a missing piece of her life had slotted quietly into place.

'Well, I'm pleased for you anyway.'

'You haven't said anything to anyone, have you?' Katrina asked, suddenly worried. Now her cousin was ecstatically happy with Theo, she was trying to make sure that everyone else was, too.

'Of course not. You told me in confidence.' Madison sighed. 'When your mum rang me the other day to find out if there was a special reason why you sounded so happy nowadays, I said it was because you loved your job and you're doing well in your exams and you're probably going to make registrar quicker than I did.'

'Thank you.' Katrina toyed with her own pizza. Though she wasn't surprised that her mother had called Madison for a quiet word. Madison's mother always called Katrina when she was concerned about Maddie, knowing they were close and always looked out for each other.

Madison reached over and squeezed her hand. 'Hey. Remember what you said to me about Theo when I was scared? You told me to hang in there because when he'd sorted out whatever the problem was in his head, he'd be worth the wait. And you were right. He was.'

'This is different.'

'It isn't different at all. It's merely that Rhys

hasn't got around to telling you what's in his head yet. And have you told him about Pete the Toad?'

'Yes. And he says my hearing's part of who I am—he doesn't have a problem with it.'

'Good. Otherwise I'd break every bone in his body. Twice,' Madison said, very coolly and very seriously.

'Maddie!' Katrina said, shocked.

'Well, I love you,' her cousin said, looking completely unrepentant. 'And anyone who hurts you has me to deal with.'

'He's not going to hurt me, Maddie.' She bit her lip. 'At least, not intentionally. But I don't want to be the first one to say how I feel,' she admitted, knowing that her confidence to her cousin would go no further. 'In case I've got it wrong.'

'For the record,' Madison said, 'I don't think you've got it wrong. He's quiet and deep, but you're the quiet one of the family so he suits you perfectly.' She smiled. 'And I'm expecting to be a bridesmaid, you know. Or matron of honour, whatever you want to call it.'

'You,' Katrina said, 'aren't just counting your chickens, you're giving them all names! But if— and I mean *if*—I ever get married, of course you're walking down the aisle behind me. Except your dress won't be pink.'

'The colour's negotiable. But I want high heels,' Madison said with an irrepressible smile.

'Anyway, we should be planning *your* wedding, not mine.'

'It isn't going to be until late spring—probably the first week of May—and we have loads of time to plan.' Madison spread her hands. 'It's the same deal. Well, almost. I can't marry Theo in a church, so you won't be walking down the aisle behind me… But you'll be there, in a dress—and very, *very* flat shoes.'

'How about a trouser suit?' Katrina suggested hopefully.

'Dress,' Madison said firmly. 'As a bridesmaid *or* a bride. But I might let you off with a trouser suit at the christening.' She paused. 'Christening. That reminds me. Christmas. We're having it at ours this year. Mum and Dad are coming down, Theo's parents are flying over from Greece, and I want you to meet them.'

Katrina looked ruefully at her. 'Sorry, hon. I'd love to be there, but I'm working on Christmas Day.'

'Early or late shift?'

'Early.'

'Good, that makes it a bit easier. Then this is how we'll do it,' Madison said. 'I'll invite Aunt Babs and Uncle Danny up for the day, too, so they get to meet Theo and his family before the wedding, and they can see you on Christmas Day instead of making do with a phone call—and you can come round to our place straight after your shift.'

'Don't hold Christmas dinner up for me,' Katrina said. 'I'll grab something on the ward. Just save me some turkey and salad for a sandwich and a big bit of Christmas cake.'

Madison laughed. 'Stop worrying. Theo's cooking, not me—and, actually, I was hoping you'd make us your special chocolate Christmas cake.'

'Course I will. But I mean it. Don't wait for me to get there before you have lunch. I'll join in when I get there.'

Madison coughed. 'Actually, the invitation was for "you" as in plural. I meant Rhys as well. Unless he's going back to Wales?'

'I'm not sure.' They hadn't discussed it. 'I'll check and let you know,' Katrina promised.

'Good. Because this is going to be the best Christmas ever,' Madison said.

Rhys could hear the screams from the other end of the ward. Quickly, he reassured his patient and his mum that he'd be back in a second, and headed straight for the sound. Katrina clearly had the same idea, because she arrived in the cubicle at the same time.

Denise—a four-year-old who'd been patched up in Theatre following a car accident and had been brought to the ward from the recovery room thirty minutes previously—was thrashing on the bed and screaming.

'All right, sweetheart. It's going to be OK,' he soothed, holding the little girl's hand.

Lynne was in the doorway. 'What happened? I did her obs five minutes ago and she was asleep.'

'My guess is she just woke up to find herself in a strange place and she's scared and she wants her mum,' Katrina said. 'Plus there was the trauma of the accident—it might just have hit her. Does anyone know the situation with her parents?'

'I'm on it. Back in a tick,' Lynne said.

'Check her notes,' Rhys said. 'Could be pain, too.'

Katrina flicked swiftly to the drug chart. 'According to this, they gave her pain relief in the recovery room. So if she's hurting…'

She didn't need to say the rest of it. They both knew that it meant Denise's injuries could be more severe than the emergency and surgical teams had thought and the little girl needed to go back into Theatre.

'Can you tell me where it hurts, *bach*?' Rhys asked.

But Denise was still wailing too much to listen to him.

'Let me give her a cuddle,' Katrina said. 'I'll tell her a story, and if I can calm her down a bit she might be able to tell us what's wrong.'

Rhys had seen how children responded to Katrina—how she'd calmed nervous and upset children on the ward before. There was something about her that made the ward feel like a still, calm place when the world was raging and spinning outside.

And that was how she made him feel, too.

So he let Katrina take his place at the little

girl's bedside and lingered a while to watch her as she cuddled the little girl and started talking to her about fairies and princesses and a magic star that could guide everyone home. Gradually, the little girl's screams subsided to noisy tears, and finally to the odd hiccuping sob as she listened to Katrina's quiet, soothing voice. Katrina rocked the little girl gently, stroking her hair and calming her.

Seeing her like that, Rhys suddenly realised the unthinkable.

He loved her.

Really loved her.

Being around Katrina was like being bathed in spring sunshine. And his world had been a much, much brighter place since she'd been in it.

Oh, lord.

This was seriously scary.

He'd never felt like this before. He didn't know how to tell Katrina—where to start, even. Though he knew that in the middle of the ward when they were looking after a distressed child definitely wasn't the right time or place.

'So can you tell me what's wrong, sweetheart?' Katrina asked. 'Does it hurt?'

'Want my mummy,' the little girl hiccuped, her lower lip wobbling.

Katrina glanced up at Rhys, her eyes full of questions.

He knew exactly what she needed to know. Whether Denise's mum was out of Theatre and when she'd be able to visit. He nodded. 'I'll go and find Lynne and see what's going on.'

He met the paediatric nurse halfway back to the reception desk. 'Any news on Denise's parents?'

'Not good,' Lynne said. 'Her mum's still in Theatre, and her dad's not answering his mobile phone.'

'How about grandparents? Aunts and uncles? A family friend, even?' he asked. 'Denise's mum must have had an emergency contact number somewhere—even if the paramedics couldn't find one on her mobile phone, maybe there was something in her diary or a notebook. Even a scrap of paper. There has to be *something*.'

'They're snowed under in the emergency department. I had a word with Eve—' one of the senior nurses in the emergency department '—and she says she'll get one of her juniors on it as soon as she can. She suggested trying the GP.'

'That's assuming we can get in touch with the GP in the first place. And even then it doesn't necessarily mean they'll have emergency contacts.' Rhys shook his head impatiently. 'Katrina's doing a brilliant job, but she can't stay with Denise indefinitely. She's due in clinic in half an hour and we don't have anyone to cover her—Will's in surgery and I'm in clinic myself. I know Tim's shadowing Katrina, but we can't chuck him in the deep end and make him do a clinic without supervision or back-up. It isn't fair to him or the patients.' And cancelling the clinic wasn't an option either.

'If Denise has bonded with Katrina, she's not going to want to let someone else take over,' Lynne said with a sigh. 'And screaming the place down really isn't going to be good for the little one, let alone the fact it'll upset the other kids.'

'She needs a familiar face,' Rhys said. And although they could probably send someone down from the ward to try and find a contact, it'd be quicker for him to do it because he could give an update on Denise's condition at the same time and answer any questions for anyone he managed to get in touch with. He folded his arms. 'I'll go down to the emergency department myself. Bleep me if you need me, warn Reception that this afternoon's clinics are going to be running late—and if there's a problem, I'll take the flak. I'll let Katrina know the situation on my way out. Can you ring Eve and tell her I'm on my way down?'

'Will do.'

'Thanks, Lynne. You're a star.' And it was good to know he could leave everything in the nurse's more than capable hands.

This was definitely a scenario where Katrina's hearing loss came into its own, he thought. Because he'd be able to mouth the message to her so the little girl didn't hear and get worried, but Katrina would be able to understand him. He dropped by the cubicle to explain the situation, then headed to the emergency department.

Eve, who'd been primed by Lynne, got Denise's mother's handbag out of the department safe for him.

'The paramedics tried the ICE number,' Eve said, referring to the 'in case of emergency' number that some people had included on their mobile phones. 'But apparently it's the same as her husband's number. There's just no reply.'

'Let's try the diary.' He flicked through the pages until he found the addresses section. 'Oh, hell. Either she hasn't written down her parents' number because she knows it off by heart, or she's not in contact with them. But there's a number here under "Nursery".' He gave Eve a relieved smile. 'That means they'll know Denise—and they're bound to have emergency contacts in addition to Denise's father.'

He managed to get through to the nursery manager and explained the situation. 'So do you have an emergency contact number we could use, please?'

'I'm sorry,' the nursery manager said, 'I can't give out a number.'

Rhys sighed. 'I rather think that a car accident ending up with a frightened little girl in a hospital bed following surgery, while her mother's still in Theatre and her father's not answering his mobile phone, counts as an emergency. Surely you can give me someone I can contact?'

'We can't give out a number,' the nursery

manager repeated. 'It's a breach of the data protection rules and we'd get into a lot of trouble.'

Rhys was very tempted to yell at the woman that sometimes rules needed to be broken, for the sake of common sense and kindness, but kept a lid on his temper. 'Then would you be prepared to call your contacts on my behalf? And, just so you know this isn't some kind of stupid prank, you can call the children's ward here and check. I imagine, as a local nursery, you'd have our number anyway—but, just in case, do you have a pen?'

'Yes.'

'Good.' Rhys gave her the number for the direct line to the ward. 'I'm Dr Rhys Morgan. Ask for me—or if I'm not back from the emergency department you can speak to the senior sister, Lynne Brearley. Right now my senior house officer's with Denise and keeping her calm, but Denise really needs someone she knows with her as soon as possible.'

'Is she going to be all right?'

'She's comfortable,' Rhys said dryly.

'Um. Data protection.'

He'd just bet the woman's face was bright red. And right at that moment he didn't have much sympathy with her. 'Indeed. Thank you for your help. And I'd appreciate it if you could call someone for Denise right now.'

When he got back to the ward, Lynne accosted him.

'I've just put the phone down to Denise's grandparents. They're on their way in,' she said. 'You're a star.'

'Hey, I'm not the one who's managed to make a little girl feel that the whole world hasn't completely collapsed on her. Our Katrina's the one who deserves the credit.'

'She's so good with the little ones. Really lights up their world,' Lynne said.

She lit up his world, too. And Rhys decided that he would tell her that night.

CHAPTER TEN

'THAT poor little girl,' Katrina said later that evening as they left the hospital. 'Just as well her grandparents are going to be able to look after her while her mum's in hospital.'

'She's going to be in for observations for a few days yet,' Rhys reminded her.

'It was lucky she was on the same side as her mum, strapped into her car seat in the back of the car rather than the front,' Katrina said. 'Ed in the emergency department told me the car was pretty much flattened on the passenger side.' They'd also learned that Denise's mother had taken the brunt of the damage, with internal injuries, a broken arm and collarbone and a broken leg.

'And why do I get the feeling that a certain doctor is going to be spending her lunch breaks taking Denise to visit her mother?' Rhys asked wryly.

Katrina spread her hands. 'You could pull rank and tell me not to.'

'You'd simply ignore me and do it anyway,' Rhys said. 'So I'm not going to waste my breath.'

'Good, you're learning.' She paused. 'Rhys, you're working on Christmas Day, too, aren't you?'

He nodded. 'It's not fair to make staff with children do it when they could be at home with their kids.'

Her view exactly. Although she missed spending the day with her family, there weren't any children to be disappointed by her absence and she usually managed either an early or a late celebration with her parents instead. 'I wondered if you were going back to Wales for Christmas.'

He shrugged. 'I'm perfectly happy here in London. Maybe we could spend the evening together after our shift.'

Part of Katrina was delighted that Rhys wanted to spend the holiday season with her, but part of her realised how estranged he was from his family, if he wasn't even planning to see them at the time of year when most people made the effort to see their families. It was a far cry from her relationship with her own family, whose closeness more than made up for its small size. She usually managed to get home once a month to see her parents, whereas Rhys hadn't returned to Wales to see his family ever since she'd known him. And as far as she knew he hadn't spoken to his parents in weeks, whereas she spoke to hers or had a conversation by text or email at least every other day.

Or maybe she'd got it wrong. Maybe this was his way of asking her to spend time with him and meet his family. 'Is your family coming up to see you in London?'

'I doubt it.'

She couldn't quite get her head around that. 'But surely they'll want to see you at Christmas?'

'I doubt it,' he said again. His voice had become very cool, warning her to leave it alone.

But how could she? If Rhys was estranged from his family, that was probably why he was so reserved, she was sure. In his shoes, barely on speaking terms with her family, she'd be utterly miserable.

So maybe she could help him heal the breach. 'How do you know unless you ask?'

He gave her an exasperated look as they

reached her front door. 'I just *do.*' He paused. 'You know what, Katrina? I think I'll go back to my place, tonight. On my own.'

On his own? Katrina felt her eyes widen. She really hadn't expected him to react like this, to push her away. 'But, Rhys—'

'Just leave it, Katrina,' he cut in quietly. 'I need some space. Not every family's like yours, you know. And some things are best left as they are. Trust me on this.'

'Rhys, I'm—'

But he'd already turned and was striding purposefully away down the street.

Katrina let herself indoors, but didn't bother cooking anything. She'd lost her appetite.

How could she have misjudged this so badly?

She was tempted to ring him, to apologise for pushing him too hard, but she had a feeling that he'd meant exactly what he'd said.

He needed space.

And the best thing she could do right now was accept that. Take him at his word. Give him what he needed.

Even though it made her miserable.

* * *

It was the first night they'd spent apart in ages. Katrina slept badly, missing the warmth of his arms round her and wishing she'd never opened her mouth. For the first time she could remember, she actually felt deaf. Cut off from everyone. Rhys was quiet, but his presence had filled the house.

She missed his music.

Missed his slow, sexy smile.

Missed *him*.

Rhys, too, spent a bad night. And although he was tempted to call Katrina as he sat drinking coffee in his kitchen at 6:00 a.m., knowing that like him she'd be awake, he also knew that she found the telephone difficult—he'd watched her at work talking to a patient's relative on the phone, pressing the earpiece as close as possible to her right ear and switching her hearing aid off in the left so she wasn't distracted by the noise of the ward.

No, a phone call wasn't the right thing to do. There was a better way. He flicked into the text service of his mobile phone and tapped out a message. *Katrina, I'm sorry. I shouldn't have snapped at you. See you at work. Will apologise properly in person. R x*

Half an hour later, his phone beeped to signal her reply. *I'm sorry too. Was too pushy. See you later. K x*

She'd added a smiley face.

So she forgave him. She'd even taken part of the blame herself, though it hadn't been her fault. That, he thought, was a lot more than he deserved.

Katrina was her usual professional self with him at work when they did the ward rounds together, and, as he'd expected she was un-available at lunchtime because she'd grabbed a chocolate bar and taken little Denise to the general ward in a wheelchair to visit her mother. Which was fine by him, because it meant he had enough time to go and buy some-thing. Strictly speaking, he knew he ought to give her a floral apology—but if he brought a huge bouquet onto the ward and then Katrina left with it, tongues would start wagging. He didn't want his personal life being the subject of hospital gossip and he knew how much she'd hated being talked about at her previous hospital when she'd split up with Pete, so he chose something rather less obvious than flowers—but something he hoped she'd like as much.

When their shifts had finished, he caught up on some paperwork while Katrina did her usual end-of-day story in the children's playroom, and timed it so that he walked out of his office at the same time that she left the playroom.

'Can I have a quick word?' he asked.

'Sure.' She allowed him to shepherd her back into his office and close the door behind them.

'I, um, wondered if I could take you to dinner at Mezze tonight. If you're not busy. To say sorry.'

'Rhys, you don't have to do that.'

'I'd like to. And I want to apologise properly… which is a bit difficult here, under the eagle eyes of our colleagues.'

'Uh-huh.'

'So are you free?'

She smiled. 'Yes. Thank you. And I'd love to go to Mezze.'

'Good.'

He waited until they were seated at the restaurant and had ordered a pile of different dishes to share—all Katrina's favourites—before he gave her the paper carrier bag.

Her eyes widened as she saw the name on the outside. 'Rhys, these are hideously expensive!'

'But you like them?'

She smiled. 'I *love* them. They're my absolute favourite chocolates—the kind of thing I buy as a birthday treat. Thank you. But you really didn't have to.'

'Yes, I did. I shouldn't have lost my temper with you last night.' He sighed. 'Not everyone has the kind of close family you do, Katrina. And I guess I'm a bit sensitive about it.'

'A *bit*?' she asked mildly.

'All right. Very,' he admitted. 'And I'm sorry.'

'I was too pushy. So I'm as much to blame, which means you really need to share these with me,' she said. Then she bit her lip. 'Um. Speaking of being pushy... Look, I understand completely if you say no, but the thing is that Maddie's having a big family Christmas do at hers. She wants me to go there as soon as I finish work on Christmas Day. My parents are coming up just for the day, because they know I normally work over the holiday—but having lunch at Maddie's is a chance for them to see me too, and to meet Theo…and…' She wriggled in her seat. 'Look, there's no pressure. If you prefer, I'll introduce you to everyone as my friend and colleague who's been on shift with me on Christmas Day. Everyone knows that Maddie, being Maddie, believes that the more the merrier. And…' She took a deep breath. 'I'm gabbling. Sorry. I just wondered if…if you'd go with me.'

She wanted him to go with her. To share a proper family Christmas. Something he hadn't had for years and years and years. Rhys had always made sure he was working over the holiday season, ever since he'd qualified, to avoid the sheer grind of the day.

A big family Christmas at Madison's with Katrina's parents, Madison's parents and Theo's family. The idea of it filled him with dread—he just wasn't used to that sort of thing. But he also knew he needed to make an effort, for Katrina's sake. Her family was important to her.

As for introducing him to them as her colleague—he knew that Madison was as close as a sister to Katrina, and he was pretty sure that

Katrina had confided in her that they were seeing each other. Even if Katrina hadn't told the rest of her family, Madison—with the best of intentions—might have already done so.

But if he wanted to be with Katrina—and he knew he did—then he was going to have to compromise. Do this one thing she'd asked of him. 'OK. I'll come.'

'Thank you.'

She held him close, and the dread started to melt away. With Katrina by his side, anything was possible. And he was beginning to believe that maybe with her he could have the relationship he'd never had in his life before. A truly loving partner and a family who'd always be there for him.

On Christmas Eve, Rhys stayed overnight at Katrina's. It unnerved him slightly—he never bothered decorating, other than putting up cards, but Katrina had gone the whole hog. A real tree which scented the air—she'd persuaded him to go with her, three days before, to choose it—covered with white twinkling lights, a holly wreath on her front door, more greenery draped round the mantelpiece, cards everywhere and candles which filled the room with Christmassy scents of orange, cloves and cinnamon. And, just for a dash of roguishness, she had a sprig of mistletoe hanging from the ceiling in the hall before the front door. 'It's not real mistletoe,' she explained, 'it's environmentally friendly silk mistletoe. But it still works the same.'

How could he resist kissing her underneath it?

After dinner—which they'd cooked together—Rhys produced a small box.

'What's this?'

'Welsh Christmas tradition—it's taffy. It's usually made on Christmas Eve, though I made it yesterday morning when I was off duty. And I set it in a tin rather than doing it the traditional way of dropping spoonfuls into ice-cold water,' he explained.

She tasted a square. 'Mmm. It's wonderful.' She tipped her head slightly to one side. 'Does it take very long to make?'

'Half an hour or so.'

'Do you know the recipe off by heart? Just, if you do…maybe we could make some to take to Maddie's tomorrow.'

Trust her to be thinking of someone else. 'Already done, *cariad*, and it's in my briefcase,' he said with a smile. 'This is only a taster for us tonight. But I can make more any time you want.'

'Rhys, I... Thank you.' She walked round to his side of the table and hugged him. 'I know it's going to be weird for you tomorrow, and I understand if you want to change your mind.'

Part of him still didn't want to go. But he really, really didn't want to hurt her by not going. 'I'll be there,' he promised.

'You're probably not going to have time to open your present from me tomorrow morning,' she said. 'So I thought maybe you might like it tonight.' She went over to a cupboard and, to his surprise, brought out a Christmas stocking. 'Happy Christmas,' she told him, kissing him lightly.

'Katrina...' There was a huge lump in his throat. When was the last time he'd had a Christmas stocking? Too long ago to remember. Though he understood why Christmas was always so difficult for his mother. The same reason why he loathed the days between Christmas and New Year, marking the anniversary of his little sister's death and the time when his life had been turned upside down and nothing had been the same again.

He pushed the memories away. Not now. Not here. Katrina clearly loved Christmas, and even though he knew he ought to tell her, he wasn't going to spoil her pleasure in the season. 'Thank you. But I didn't make you a stocking.'

She shrugged. 'That's OK. I wasn't expecting anything.'

'I did buy you something,' he said. Though he'd cheated, putting the presents in a Christmas gift bag or having them wrapped in the shop. 'Wait.' He retrieved them from his overnight bag. 'Happy Christmas, *cariad*,' he said.

'Thank you,' she said, kissing him. 'Let's open them one at a time.'

She loved the film encyclopaedia he'd bought her, the digital photo frame, the new restored special edition of one of her favourite films, a large box of the exclusive chocolates he'd bought her previously as an apology and the only girly indulgence he knew she liked—some exclusive chocolate-scented toiletries.

And he was blown away by what she'd given him. Inside the stocking was an envelope containing a year's membership to the British Film Institute, a CD by one of his favourite cellists, seasonally shaped chocolates which she'd wrapped individually, and a tiny musical box that played the first part of Bach's Air on a G String. And a rare first edition of one of his favourite Cornell Woolrich tales—something that had been missing from his collection. 'Katrina, I've no idea where you managed to find this, but it's fabulous. And you're wonderful,' he said, meaning it.

The following morning saw Rhys dressed up as Father Christmas, Katrina and Tim as Santa's helpers—both in elf costumes—and Lynne as a Christmas fairy, complete with wings and a magic wand. Thanks to the Hospital Friends Group, they had small parcels to give out to all the children on the ward and their siblings: a touch-and-feel board book and socks for the babies; colouring pencils and joke books for the older ones; and small gift tokens for the over-tens to put towards music or video games.

Katrina noticed that little Tommy Price, in with idiopathic thrombocytopetic purpura—a condition involving bruising and a rash that didn't disappear when pressed, showing that there was bleeding under the skin, and they were busy checking out the cause—didn't have any visitors. Although he'd said thank you for the present from Father Christmas, the eight-year-old hadn't moved from his bed to join the other children in the playroom. And she'd noticed that although all the other children in the bay had cards stuck to the wall above their beds, Tommy had nothing.

Her heart ached for him. Seeing how the other children's families had made a special fuss of them must have made him realise what he was missing, and as a result he'd withdrawn completely.

Was this how Rhys's childhood had been, too? And, if so, was he going to be able to cope with a Gregory family Christmas? she wondered.

She stopped by Tommy's bed. His family had been the only ones not to respond to her request for permission to give all the patients a seasonal chocolate lolly. She'd decided to take the line that silence indicated consent, so she handed Tommy the reindeer-shaped chocolate with the red nose. 'Hey. Happy Christmas,' she said.

'Yeah. You, too. And thanks,' he added swiftly.

Tommy's eyes were a little too bright; Katrina, realising that he was near tears, began telling him atrocious jokes until she made him smile. She made a point of pulling a Christmas cracker with him at lunch and slipping him an extra chocolate lolly at the end of her shift.

'I can't believe Tommy Price's family didn't even bother coming to visit him on Christmas Day,' she said to Rhys, glowering as they left the hospital together. 'That's so *mean*.'

'Don't you think you're being just a tiny a bit judgemental?' Rhys asked mildly. 'Maybe his parents are desperately scared of hospitals. Maybe home life's tough—maybe his parents are caring for an elderly parent or a small child with special needs as well, and there just aren't enough hours in the day.'

'You're right. I'm sorry.' She sighed. 'But sometimes I really wish I had a magic wand. I don't want fabulous riches or eternal youth.'

'You just want to fix things for people,' he finished. 'But you can't fix everything, *cariad*.'

'No. I just wish I could.' She shook herself. 'Right. Enough. We're going to Maddie's.'

* * *

The nearer they got to Madison and Theo's house, the more Rhys's stomach churned with nerves. This was important to Katrina, and he was going to do it. But, lord, how he wished he were on a desert island instead. Especially when Madison ushered them inside and he realised how many people were there, how everyone was talking and laughing and acting as if they'd known each other all their lives despite the fact that, as far as he knew, this was the first time Theo's family had met the Gregorys.

This was so very different from the way he was used to spending Christmas.

He managed to smile and be polite to everyone, and Madison seemed pleased with the home-made Welsh taffy and the champagne he'd brought as his contribution to the day. She was definitely delighted with the chocolate Christmas cake Katrina had made; clearly Katrina's love of chocolate was shared by her family.

He found himself a quiet place on the edge of the room, but from the moment they arrived Katrina was right in the centre of things, clearly a much-loved part of the family. But the more he watched, the more he realised how close everyone was. Katrina's parents finished each other's sentences. Madison's parents kept catching each other's eye and smiling. Theo's family, being Greek, were noisily and openly affectionate with everyone, and Theo fussed over his pregnant fiancée.

Katrina's mum was doing her best to make him feel welcome, talking to him about his job—though he noticed that she avoided the normal questions about missing his family at Christmas, so he had a feeling that Katrina had primed her parents not to ask.

Katrina.

Although he responded politely enough to her family, he couldn't keep his eyes off her. She was reading a story to Theo's niece and cuddling Theo's nephew, sitting on the floor by the Christmas tree and looking as if she belonged.

Well, of course she belonged. This was her family.

She fitted into the extended family, too. She'd fit in anywhere. Even his mother, Rhys thought, would find it hard to resist her.

And then it hit him.

Between them, the three sets of parents had clocked up close to a century of happy marriage. They'd support their children, help them through any rough patches so their marriages would work, too.

And their love was unconditional.

So maybe, just maybe, he could afford to take the risk with Katrina. If Katrina was willing to take the risk with him.

He was still mulling it over when Theo's niece came over to him. 'You come and have a story too,' she said in accented but perfect English, taking his hand.

How could he resist following her over to the Christmas tree?

Though Rhys was aware of a very weird feeling in the region of his heart when he sat down next to Katrina and little Arianna insisted that he cuddle her baby brother, Petros, while she and Katrina did a puppet show with her new toys.

Rhys was used to cuddling babies and children. He did it all the time at work, to soothe them when they were in pain or to explain what was going to happen next in their treatment. So holding a toddler shouldn't make him feel so odd—a feeling he couldn't pin down.

'Sorry,' Katrina mouthed.

'It's fine,' he mouthed back, and settled back with the toddler, making appropriate noises of appreciation during the puppet show.

To his surprise, he found himself relaxing and enjoying the whole family thing. Pulling crackers and telling terrible jokes, laughing at the even more terrible ones Theo's niece had clearly learned especially, and mucking in with everyone to set the table for tea and clear up afterwards and play charades.

And then finally it was time to leave.

Katrina's mother hugged him goodbye, Katrina's father shook his hand warmly, Theo clapped him on the shoulder, Theo's family all hugged him—but Madison was the one who floored him. 'Thank you for coming,' she said, holding him close. And then she added in a voice so low it was clearly not meant to be heard by anyone else, 'And especially for doing this for Kat. She's special.'

Yeah. He knew that.

'And I think you are too,' Madison added, 'if you'll let yourself.'

He knew then without a doubt that Katrina had confided in her cousin—a confidence Madison had kept. Given how close they were, he had a feeling that Madison was very protective about her younger cousin. So the fact she thought he was good enough for Katrina…

He had a lump in his throat for a good five minutes after they left.

'I'm sorry. Was it so awful?' Katrina asked when they were on the tube.

'No. Your family's lovely.'

'I'm glad you liked them.' She bit her lip. 'Just…you've been a bit quiet since we left.'

'I was a bit overwhelmed,' he admitted. 'It's not the kind of thing I'm used to.' And right then he didn't want to tell her what Madison had said. He was still trying to come to terms with it himself. The feeling that this woman was so right for him, that she was the one he wanted in his life.

But there were a few things he needed to sort out before he could ask her to share his life—to take the risk with him.

She curled her fingers round his. 'Thanks, anyway.'

'Any time.'

She smiled. 'So does that mean I can ask you to come to Maddie's wedding with me next May?'

Wedding.

He took a deep breath. 'Sure.'

'Good.' She paused. 'I told her about your cello. And we were kind of wondering…it's going to be a civil wedding, not a church do, so she won't have an organist to accompany her down the aisle. And…'

He guessed what she wanted to ask but was clearly holding back. 'You want me to play the cello at her wedding?'

'Only if you want to. Not if it's going to be…' She paused. 'If it's going to be difficult for you.'

Being part of her family? Rhys stopped, spun her round to face him and brushed his mouth over hers. 'If you want me to play, of course I'll do it. Tell her to pick whatever she likes—no, I'll tell her that myself. Just as long as I have time to practise and polish any pieces I don't already know.'

He'd go to her cousin's wedding. Play the cello during the ceremony. Let her family draw him into the charmed circle.

And maybe, just maybe, he'd ask Katrina a question of his own. In the new year. When he'd sorted out a few things in his head.

CHAPTER ELEVEN

THE first hurdle was two days before New Year. A day Rhys loathed. Even after all these years, he found his skin always was a bit too thin on that day. The anniversary of his little sister Gwyneth's death. He knew he ought to tell Katrina about it, but he just didn't have the words. Maybe tomorrow, he told himself, when things were less raw again. And he managed to act as if things were completely normal—until the middle of his shift, when a six-week-old baby was admitted with pneumonia.

The coincidence was harsh enough, but it was one he'd faced before and knew he could deal with. What he couldn't deal with was what happened right at the end of his shift—when the baby's mother, clearly worried sick, was shouting at her little boy. Blaming him for bringing home the virus that had made little

Felicity ill and caused her to be susceptible enough to pick up pneumonia on top of it. The little boy's face was white, pinched, and he was weeping silently.

And Rhys, remembering the child he'd been and the way he'd felt, was furious. He just about kept a lid on his temper as he strode into the cubicle. 'Problem?' he asked abruptly.

Mrs Walters stared at him, clearly shocked at the way he'd walked straight in, but the stethoscope hanging round his neck and his hospital ID card pinned to his shirt told her she was dealing with a senior doctor—one who wouldn't be fobbed off. Though she was obviously too angry to let it check her. 'Of course there's a problem! My daughter's lying there, seriously ill. You've got eyes, haven't you?'

Rhys wasn't bothered by her rudeness, but he was bothered by the little boy's tears. Today of all days. He was aware that his fists were clenched in anger, and deliberately flexed his hands. 'I think,' he said carefully, 'we need a word in my office.' He glanced around— luckily Lynne was in the bay opposite. 'Lynne?' he said to the nurse. 'Can you do me a favour and keep an eye on Felicity and her brother for me?'

'Simon's not going anywhere,' the woman said.

'No, but you and I are. And your little boy's already upset—he doesn't need to hear this,' he said.

Mrs Walters's face whitened—clearly she thought he was going to tell her something drastic about Felicity's condition. And although Rhys knew he ought to do the decent thing and reassure her before they went left Felicity's cubicle, right at that moment he wasn't feeling particularly nice. Not after the way the woman had treated her little boy. It was too close to his own childhood experience. So he merely shepherded her to his office and closed the door behind them.

'Mrs Walters, I realise you're upset because Felicity's ill, but shouting at your son isn't going help make her better. She needs quiet and rest—as do the other children on the ward.'

She lifted her chin, looking belligerent. 'Don't you talk to me like that,' she said. 'I'm going to report you.'

'You do that,' Rhys said, knowing it was an empty threat—he'd done nothing wrong. 'But I suggest you focus your thoughts a little closer to home first. Felicity should recover without any lasting effects, though she's likely to pick up coughs and colds a bit more easily than most little ones for the next year or so. So although it's worrying for you, seeing her in here—and she'll get a little bit worse before she improves, because that's the nature of the disease—she'll be on the mend very soon.' He folded his arms. 'What I'm concerned about is your little boy. Even though we try to make our ward as comfortable as possible for children, the hospital's still a very scary place for them. Simon's already worried about his baby sister, seeing her here in hospital. You've shouted at him and told him that it's all his fault, so he's probably feeling scared and guilty as well right now.'

Mrs Walters said nothing, but her face went a very dull red.

'I might add that it's highly unlikely Felicity caught the virus from her brother—a virus tends to do the rounds and spread very quickly. She could have caught it from a dozen or more different people. So right now I think your son needs a bit of reassurance—a hug from his mum—and to know that he's loved.' Something he hadn't had at Simon's age—though he was old enough to be over that.

Mrs Walters glared at him, but he could see the guilt starting as his words sank in. Even though he wanted to yell at her, he was aware of his reasons, and reined himself in. Time to be kind. Show a bit of sympathy, he reminded himself. Do what Katrina, with her warmth and sweetness, would do. 'And I think you'll find it'll help you, too. Because Simon will hug you back and give you a bit of comfort in return.' Katrina had taught him the power of a hug.

Mrs Walters's face crumpled and she burst into tears.

Oh, lord. He'd wanted to stop her yelling at her little boy, but this hadn't been quite what he'd intended. Awkwardly, Rhys took the box of tissues from his desk and offered it to her. And when she'd calmed down again, he took her back to the ward.

He'd expected Lynne to be sitting with Simon and Felicity, but instead the little boy was sitting on Katrina's lap.

'Thanks for looking after Simon for us,' he said to Katrina.

'No problem. We've had a lovely time.' She smiled back at him. 'And Felicity's holding her own.'

'Good.' Rhys crouched down so he was at the little boy's height. 'Are you all right there, Simon?' he asked softly.

The little boy nodded, wide-eyed. 'Dr Katrina told me a story.'

'She's really good at that.' Rhys ruffled his hair. 'Hey, I know it's a bit scary, seeing your baby sister here with all these tubes and wires and machines beeping, but she's going to be absolutely fine. And I want you to know that it's not your fault your sister caught pneumonia.'

'Mummy said…' The little boy's lower lip wobbled.

'Your mummy was very worried and scared, just like you are, and sometimes people say things they don't mean when they're worried and scared,' Rhys said. 'But I'm a doctor. My job is to make people better, and I'm going to make Felicity better. Your mummy understands that now. And it really isn't your fault. It's the time of year when there are lots of bugs about, and Felicity's very little, so she can't fight the bugs as well as you and I can.'

The little boy dragged in a breath. 'So she's not going to die?'

'She's not going to die.' Not like Gwyneth had. Advances in medicine would make sure of that. 'All those tubes and wires you can see are there to help her breathe more easily, to help her get enough food, and so we can keep an eye on her and give her medicine when we need to, to make her better,' Rhys said gently. 'And she's not the only one in the ward like this. There are five other babies in this bay who have a similar sort of thing to your sister. Some are more poorly, and some are a bit better because they got the bugs a bit earlier than Felicity did and they're already on the mend.'

The little boy nodded, but said nothing.

'I think your mummy wants a word,' he said, and looked at Mrs Walters.

She followed his lead and crouched down by the little boy, hugging him. 'I'm sorry I shouted at you, Simon. Dr Morgan's right. I was worried and I took it out on you and that was wrong of me. It isn't your fault—and I do love you. I really do.'

Rhys gave an approving nod—and then walked quietly to the safety of his office, knowing that he needed five minutes to himself before he could face the ward again.

Something was definitely wrong, Katrina thought. Even though Rhys had been perfectly in control and hadn't even raised his voice, she'd seen something in his eyes. And he'd been even quieter than usual for the last couple of days.

She went to his office, and blinked in surprise. Since when had Rhys shut his office door?

Worried, she knocked on the door, but she also walked in without waiting for him to say anything and closed the door behind her.

'You're not all right, so don't tell me you are,' she said, seeing the expression on his face. 'What's happened?'

He turned away; she was fairly sure he said something but she didn't quite catch it. 'I can't hear you, Rhys. You were mumbling and I couldn't see your mouth to read what you just said. Please, can you look at me and repeat that?' she asked, her voice soft but clear.

He looked at her. 'Nothing. It's not important.'

This time she wasn't going to let him off the hook. 'It's not nothing,' she said. 'And it *is* important.'

'I don't want to talk about it here.'

That last word gave her hope. It meant he was going to open up to her. Not at the hospital—but there was a real chance that he'd talk to her. 'Look, you should've been off duty twenty minutes ago and so should I. Let's go back to my place. It's quiet and we won't be disturbed.'

To her relief, he agreed.

He was silent all the way back to her house; she respected it, not pushing him to talk about the situation in public. But as soon as they were in her kitchen and he was sitting at the table with a mug of coffee in his hands, she directed, 'Talk to me, Rhys.'

He sighed. 'I just let a case get to me.'

'Felicity Walters?'

He nodded.

'Even I could hear her mother yelling—from the other side of the ward, at that.' She gritted her teeth. 'I was just on my way over to see if I could sort it out when I saw you'd beaten me to it. And

I don't know how on earth you got her to apologise to him, but you were brilliant.'

'Mmm.'

His voice was flat, and she frowned. 'There's more to it than that, isn't there?'

He twisted the mug round and round on the table. 'Yes.' He was silent for a long, long moment, and then he looked up at her. 'I was about the same age as young Simon when my little sister Gwyneth was taken to hospital with pneumonia.'

But he'd said he was an only child.

Her questions must have shown in her face, because he said quietly, 'Gwynnie wasn't so lucky.'

'Oh, Rhys.' She put her mug down, went over to him and held him close.

He shifted so that he could pull her onto his lap. 'You're the only thing that stopped me wanting to strangle that woman. Because you've taught me the power of a hug,' he said.

His voice sounded slightly thick, and Katrina could feel tears in her own eyes. 'I'm so sorry.'

'Not your fault.' He dragged in a breath. 'Though I can remember my mother yelling at me the same way Simon's mother yelled at him. Blaming me for bringing the virus home. If it hadn't been for me, Gwyneth wouldn't have got pneumonia and she wouldn't have died.'

She pulled back just far enough so she could look into his eyes. 'Rhys, you're a paediatrician. You *know* that's not true.'

'I know that now,' he agreed tonelessly. 'But I believed it for a long time when I was a child.'

No wonder he wasn't close to his parents. Did they still blame him? Katrina wondered. 'When did it happen?' she asked.

'Twenty-eight years ago.'

She had a nasty feeling he meant *exactly* twenty-eight years ago. 'It's the anniversary today?' she guessed.

He nodded. 'Any other day, I can deal with it. Today, I was close to losing it and acting incredibly unprofessionally. I was so angry I nearly threw her out of the ward myself.'

'But you didn't,' she said fiercely. 'You rose above it. You understood what drove her to do it and you fixed it. And I'm so proud of you for that.'

His eyes were suspiciously bright as he looked at her. 'Are you, now?'

'Yes.' She nodded furiously. 'And now I understand why you've been quiet, the last few days.'

'I should've told you before. Explained,' Rhys said. 'But...' He broke off.

'You're a very private man. You don't like talking about things.' She bit her lip. 'And I've been nagging you. I pushed you into coming with me to Maddie's for Christmas. Pushed you about playing the cello for her wedding. I'm so—'

'Shh.' He pressed a forefinger to her lips. 'Don't apologise. It's OK. You pushed me, yes, but you did me a favour. You showed me what a real family Christmas is like.'

'You mean, you never...?' She stared at him, stunned.

'Not since I was three. And I can barely remember that.' He grimaced. 'As I said, my parents split up when I was just about to start school. The Christmas when Gwynnie was in hospital was our last together.' He shrugged. 'I guess it's hard for a relationship to survive a loss like that.'

She thought about it. Would her parents have got through it? Would Madison's?

And she was absolutely sure of the answer. 'If you love someone enough, you'll get through it together. I'm not saying it'd be easy, and it would take an awful lot of work, but you'd help each other through it. One of you would have a strong day when the other wasn't so strong, and vice versa. You'd get through it with teamwork.'

'I don't think my parents loved each other enough,' Rhys said. 'And there were problems before my sister died. I remember them shouting a lot. Especially my dad. But then I remember them telling me I was going to have a little brother or sister and the shouting stopped for a bit after that.' He swallowed hard. 'I was so pleased at the thought of being a big brother. Having someone to play with. I had cousins, but we weren't close—not like you and Maddie. My dad didn't see much of his family. And I think he was going through a bad time at work. There were a lot of rows, and then suddenly he was home all the time...' Rhys shook his head. 'Looking back as an adult, I realise that was probably when the mine closed.'

'Your dad lost his job?' Katrina asked.

'Along with most of the men in the village, so

it was pretty rough on everyone. Especially around Christmas, when they were upset at not being able to afford to give their kids the presents they'd wanted to buy and worried about how they were going to manage and where they were going to find work.' He sighed. 'And, again, looking back with an adult's wisdom and knowing what I do now about medicine, all the stress probably sent my mum into labour early.'

'Very early?'

'Six weeks.' He shrugged. 'And you know as well as I do that's enough for a baby to be more prone to picking up a respiratory infection—and struggling more with it than a full-term baby. And then I came home from nursery with a really terrible cold.' He dragged in a breath. 'Gwynnie picked it up. The doctor said it was just a cold, but she got worse and worse. She couldn't breathe properly.'

'RSV?' Katrina guessed. Respiratory syncytial virus was one that most children had had by school age—and it was practically epidemic at this time of year. In older children and adults it tended to appear as a really heavy cold, but babies often really struggled. As Rhys had explained to Felicity's brother, the bay where little Felicity was being treated was full of babies who'd tested positive for the virus.

'Probably,' he said, his voice still flat. 'And it turned to pneumonia.'

Just like Felicity's case. It must have hurt a lot every time he walked into the bay or saw the little girl's name on the board, bringing back painful memories from his past.

'The doctor sent her to hospital, but it was too late. She died two days later.'

With premature babies, doctors were taught to err on the side of caution, but clearly it hadn't happened in Gwyneth's case. 'Why on earth didn't your family doctor send her to hospital earlier?'

'Think about it. You're a GP. It's coming up to Christmas. Everyone in the village has got a stinking cold, half of them think their cold's so bad that they need antibiotics—even when they don't—and you're rushed off your feet because of all the people coming to see you with stress-related symptoms since the mine closed and half the men in the village lost their jobs. That, or they're coming to you, telling you in private that their husbands are depressed but refuse to come and see you, and asking what you can do to help men who are too proud to admit they need help. You're swamped and you don't know which way to turn next. Of course you're going to miss things.' He pulled her closer. 'And that's what I think happened.'

She shook her head in amazement. 'You're incredible, Rhys. If I'd lost Maddie like that…it doesn't bear thinking about. I don't think I could ever forgive the doctor.'

'Understanding isn't *quite* the same as forgiving,' he admitted.

'And that woman today… In your shoes, I think I would've strangled her.'

'No, you wouldn't.' He brushed his mouth against hers, very briefly. 'Because you're warm and sweet and nice. And if it wasn't for you, I probably would've lost my temper with her and chucked her bodily off the ward.'

'What do you mean, if it wasn't for me?'

'You taught me the power of a hug,' he said simply.

She swallowed hard. 'Oh, Rhys.'

'I'm just glad you're in my life.'

She reached up to kiss him. 'And I'm glad

you're in mine. I know it's been hard for you, telling me. But I'm glad you did. And I want you to know I'm here for you.'

'I know. And I appreciate it.'

She stroked his face. 'So that's why you chose medicine over music? Why you work stupid hours?'

'So other families don't have to go through what mine did, you mean?' He looked thoughtful. 'Probably. I know it wasn't my fault, but I do sometimes wonder, what if? What if she hadn't caught that virus and died: would things have been different?'

'Do you think they would have been?'

He wrinkled his nose. 'I doubt it. I think Gwynnie's death was the catalyst for my parents splitting up, but if she'd lived then they would've split up over something else.'

Katrina was pretty sure of the answer, but she asked the question anyway. 'Have you ever talked to your family about it?'

'No.'

'How long is it since you saw them?'

He shrugged. 'I can't remember when I last saw my father. We haven't exchanged Christmas or birthday cards for quite a while.' He paused. 'He remarried and had three more girls, so I guess he didn't need me around.'

'Rhys, you're his firstborn. Of course he still needed you around.'

'I'm a reminder of bad times for him. Just like I am for my mother.'

'Do you still see her?'

'I visit her every few months, but I don't stay long.' He shrugged. 'It's hard for her, Katrina.'

'It's been hard for you, too,' she pointed out.

'I'm not a little boy any more. I can deal with things. But now you know the truth about my family. They're not like yours, Katrina.'

And she was very, very glad hers hadn't been like that. 'I wish for your sake they'd been more like mine.'

'So,' he said softly, 'do I. But you can't change the past, and I really don't want to drag it up any more.'

'Of course. And thank you for being honest with me.'

'Honest?' He smiled ruefully. 'Not quite. Because there's something I've wanted to say to you for a while.'

Her heart missed a beat. No. She was sitting on his lap, he was holding her close…he couldn't be about to end things between them. Surely not.

Please not.

'What might that be?' she asked.

He raked a hand through his hair. 'I've never said this to anyone before. And there are bits of me that are scared to say it. In case I get it wrong. And my timing's completely out.'

She couldn't read his face at all. And for him to be awkward and unsure… She was starting to worry. But if her world was about to crash down, better to know sooner than later. She lifted her chin. 'Be brave.' Even though she didn't feel brave—at all. 'Say it straight out.'

'I love you,' he said.

She stared at him, hardly able to take it in. 'Did you just say…?'

'Sorry. I told you it was bad timing. I've already dumped enough on you tonight.' He turned his face away.

'No, no, no.' Gently, she cupped his face with both hands and made sure he was looking straight at her. 'Guess what? I love you, too.'

He was silent for a long, long time. And then he said, 'I can't remember the last time anyone said that to me.'

What? She'd been told every single day for her entire life—either in person, or by text, or by phone, or by a card, or by something daft one of her parents had spotted on a day out, decided she'd like and parcelled up for her. It was something she did for her family too—she and Madison often gave each other 'unbirthday' presents, whether it was a fridge magnet or sticky notes or just a postcard one thought would amuse the other.

How could someone never be told they were loved?

It was way outside her comprehension.

'What about your ex-girlfriends?' she asked.

He shrugged. 'I told you, I've never said it before. I couldn't trust myself to commit—I've never had much faith in family and relationships—and my last few girlfriends said I was too cold.'

'You're not cold at all,' Katrina said. 'You're private, yes, but you're warm and you're clever and you're sexy as hell. And I love you.'

'This isn't fair of me. You deserve to be part

of a warm, loving family, and I can't give you that,' he warned.

'You don't need to,' she said simply. 'I already have one. And I'd be happy to share them with you.'

There was wonder in his face as he looked at her. 'I never thought this could happen to me. I love you, Katrina. I think I have since the moment I met you. When you went all stroppy on me and informed me that you were going to put a bit of sunshine into a child's life and nobody was going to stop you.' He smiled. 'You've put sunshine back into my life.'

'Good. And I intend to keep it that way.' She paused. 'There's this little thing called teamwork. And I happen to think we make a great team.'

'Yes. We do.' He kissed her. A sweet, gentle kiss that was full of promise—a kiss that told her he'd finally broken down the wall around his heart and let her in.

It didn't stop at a kiss. And Katrina didn't protest when Rhys carried her up the stairs to her bedroom. Right at that moment, she knew they both needed the ultimate closeness.

Afterwards, she lay curled in his arms.

'I love you.' He stole a kiss. 'And I'm going to tell you every day.'

'I'll hold you to that.' She smiled at him. 'And I'm going to tell you, too.'

'Good. I've just discovered I quite like the sentence. Though I might need some practice in hearing it.'

She grinned. 'That sounds like a hint. I love you, Rhys Morgan.'

He smiled, but there was a hint of sadness in his eyes.

'You know, my parents liked you, too. They thought you were a little bit quiet, but I'm the quiet and dreamy one of the family—so as far as they're concerned you match me.'

'Katrina Gregory, no *way* are you quiet,' Rhys said, laughing. 'A quiet person wouldn't perform a glove-puppet story every day in the children's playroom.'

She chuckled. 'I didn't say I was quiet. I said I'm the quiet one *in my family*. There's a difference. They're noisy and bouncy, but they respect that I'm not quite as full on as the rest of them and they still love me. They still value me for who I am. And they'll value you, too. Just as I do.'

He shifted so he could kiss her. 'I love you, Katrina Gregory. And thank you. For...' His words caught in his throat.

'You'd do the same for me,' Katrina said confidently. 'And everything's going to be fine. Because we'll have great teamwork.'

'This isn't all I want to say to you, you know.' He stroked her face. 'There's more. But I need to tie up some loose ends first. Sort out some things that should've been sorted out a long, long time ago.' He kissed her gently. 'And then I can start the new year exactly as I mean to go on.'

CHAPTER TWELVE

THE following day, Rhys was doing the ward round. Felicity's mother was sitting next to the baby's crib and looked up when he took the notes from the basket at the end of the bed.

'Dr Morgan? There's an extra tube up her nose today. And it's taped to her face. Doesn't it…?' She bit her lip.

He guessed immediately what she wasn't saying. 'Hurt? No, it doesn't—the tape means it stays in place and she can't accidentally pull it out.' He sat down next to her. 'It's a lot easier for her having oxygen going through the tube up her nose than having a mask on. What it does is help her to breathe more easily, and that in turn means she'll be less tired. I know it looks pretty scary, but the tube isn't hurting her at all. She's holding her own.'

She nodded, clearly too overcome to speak.

'How's Simon?' he asked.

Tears glittered in Mrs Walters's eyes. 'Last night he told me he wished it was Christmas again, so Santa would bring his little sister home.'

Rhys felt a huge lump blocking his throat. When Gwyneth had died, he could remember doing exactly the same thing—begging Santa to come back and bring Gwyneth with him, and he'd never ask for another toy, ever again.

'You'd be surprised how quickly they bond,' he said gruffly. 'But Felicity's doing fine. We've got her temperature back under control, she's on amoxycillin to sort out the bacterial infection, and because we're feeding her by tube she doesn't have to work so hard and wear herself out drinking her milk.' He smiled at her. 'I'd say she'll be able to manage without the extra oxygen in a day or two, and she'll be back home with you next week, but that cough might linger for a couple of months. And you'll probably find her feeding schedule's gone right back to how it was when she was born,' he warned. 'I'm afraid you'll be up a couple of times a night with her until she's back in a routine again.'

'I can live with that, as long as she's all right.'

'So Simon's not with you today?'

'His dad's taken him to the football to cheer him up a bit. He drew her a picture, though.' She took a sheet of paper from her handbag and unfolded it.

Exactly the kind of drawings Rhys remembered doing at that age. Stick people representing his family. *Mummy, Daddy, me and Flisty,* written in a careful childish script. 'That's lovely.'

'Yeah.' She sniffed. 'And I'm sorry I yelled at you yesterday.'

'You were under a lot of stress. Don't worry about it. It's forgotten,' Rhys said. He checked Felicity, then stroked her cheek. 'Give her a day or two and she'll be off oxygen. But you can pick her up and give her a cuddle, and when she's strong enough to manage without the tubes you can feed her. She's doing fine.'

Later that evening, Katrina was at home, trying and failing to concentrate on the film encyclopaedia Rhys had bought her for Christmas. Rhys was at his own flat, calling his parents. She tried not to feel hurt that he'd chosen to make the calls alone and hadn't invited her to be with him, but he was a private man and she knew it. And he'd said he needed to sort out a few things. There was probably a lot he hadn't told her about his past.

'Stop being so needy,' she told herself fiercely. 'He's told you he loves you. And he's never said that to anyone. It should be enough.'

Then her doorbell rang. When she opened the door, she was surprised to see Rhys on the doorstep, carrying a huge bouquet of flowers and a bottle of champagne.

'Happy new year, *cariad*,' he said with a smile, handing her the flowers.

She let him in. 'But I wasn't expecting…'

'It's New Year's Eve. A time for looking back and a time for looking forward. I was hoping I might be able to spend it with you.'

Tears pricked her eyes. 'I thought…' She'd thought that she wasn't going to see him that evening.

'I love you, Katrina,' he said softly. 'I know I didn't ask you to be there when I called my parents, but I wasn't pushing you away. I was trying to protect you in case things turned nasty.

After years of avoiding each other and not talking…I thought it might be awkward, and I didn't want you upset.' He retrieved the flowers from her arms and set them on the floor, along with the champagne, and held her close.

'So how did it go?'

He sighed. 'My mum…well, she is as she is. I don't think even you could thaw her out, *cariad*,' he admitted.

'How about your dad?'

'He'd moved. But luckily the person who bought his house was a friend of his, and gave me his new number.' Rhys paused. 'I'm going to see him on Saturday.'

'Good. Because I think you both need to talk.'

'Yes. He sounded a bit…well, guarded.'

'You probably did, too,' she pointed out. 'And if it's been a long time since you've spoken…'

'It has.' He drew in a breath. 'Katrina, I know it's a lot to ask, and you probably already have plans to see your family this weekend, but I was wondering… Will you come to Wales with me?'

'Of course I will.' There was a lump in her throat which made her words sound husky.

'Are you sure?'

She nodded. 'You're asking me to meet your family. So of course I'll go, Rhys.'

'Don't take it personally if they're funny with you,' he warned.

'I won't.' She slid her hands round his neck and drew his mouth down to hers. 'I have you. Anything else is a bonus.'

His arms tightened round her. 'How did I get to be so lucky?'

'I think,' she said, 'Fate owes you big-time.' She glanced at her watch. 'In a couple of hours, it'll be the new year.'

'Did you want to go to a party?'

They'd had enough invitations. And turned them down. She shook her head. 'Lots of noise, low light and drunken people slurring their words and not moving their mouths properly when they speak isn't a good combination for me. Besides, we're both on duty tomorrow.'

'Then I have an idea.' He kissed again her, then disentangled himself from her arms and retrieved the champagne. 'You, me, this and bed…and the first thing I'm going to say to you in the new year is "I love you".'

And he did.

* * *

The following Saturday, Rhys drove them to visit his father. Katrina noted that the nearer they drew to Wales, the less he spoke, and she could see the strain in his face as he drove over the Severn Bridge.

She placed a hand on his thigh. 'Is it that bad, coming home?'

'Land of my fathers, and all that?' He wrinkled his nose. 'Yes. But it needs to be done.' He glanced at the clock. 'We still have a way to go—so as it's practically lunchtime I vote we stop at the next decent-looking pub.'

'Sure.'

The pub in question turned out to have a real open fire, delighting her. And according to the menu all the food was from locally sourced ingredients. 'This looks fantastic, but there are loads of local specialities here and I can't choose between them. As it's your part of the world, what do you recommend?' she asked.

'I'm torn between Glamorgan sausages with mash and red onion marmalade, and lamb cawl.'

His accent had grown more pronounced, she noticed, a soft lilt. Even sexier than normal. 'I'll have whichever of the two you don't have, and we'll share tastes,' she said.

He smiled. 'Fabulous idea.' He went to the bar and ordered their meals and a drink, the food was every bit as good as Katrina had expected, but by the time they'd finished eating and were back on the road, she had a huge knot in her stomach. 'I think I'm beginning to realise how you felt, meeting my family,' she admitted.

'A bit overwhelmed, *cariad*?' he asked softly. 'Don't worry. It won't be that bad. Remember, it's teamwork—we're in this together.'

And then at last he parked outside a small cottage. 'Ready?'

Katrina took his hand and squeezed it. 'Ready.'

'Then let's do this.' Rhys took a deep breath, got out of the car, and opened Katrina's door for her. He was aware that his heart rate was speeding up with every step he took nearer to the door, and his stomach was churning. Llewellyn had sounded so guarded on the phone. So did he actually *want* to see his son, or had he only agreed to see Rhys out of some sense of duty?

There was only one way to find out.

He knocked on the door.

Moments later, it was opened by a man who could have been his double, only twenty-five years older and with iron-grey hair rather than dark.

'Hello,' Llewellyn Morgan said softly.

Diffidently, Rhys held out his hand. Llewellyn grasped it firmly, then shook his head and pulled Rhys into his arms. 'My son,' he said, holding Rhys close. His voice was cracked with emotion, and Rhys knew at that moment he'd spent a quarter of a century living a lie. Because the man who held him close, tears choking his voice, was a man who really did want to see his son. Duty had nothing to do with the reason why Llewellyn had agreed to see him today.

'My manners.' Llewellyn shook himself. 'I shouldn't leave you standing here on the doorstep. Come in.'

'Thanks. This is Katrina,' Rhys said.

'It's good to meet you, *cariad*,' Llewellyn said, shaking Katrina's hand.

'You, too,' Katrina said.

'This is Dilys, my wife,' Llewellyn said, beckoning the woman who sat quietly on the sofa, waiting.

'Pleased to meet you,' Katrina said politely.

'And you.' Dilys placed a hand across her heart. 'And Rhys. You're the spit of your father when he was your age. When I first met him.' She flapped her hand. 'Oh, listen to me rabbiting on, and you've come all this way to see us. Can I get you a cup of tea? Coffee?'

'Coffee for me, please. Black, no sugar,' Rhys said. 'Katrina?'

'White, no sugar, please,' she said. 'And can I help you, Dilys?'

Rhys knew exactly what Katrina was doing. Giving him time with his father. And the smile she sent him as she followed Dilys made his heart swell.

'I hoped against hope you'd see me one day,' Llewellyn said when Dilys and Katrina had left the room. 'Though I thought that was it when you stopped sending cards.'

'When *I* stopped sending cards?' Rhys asked. 'Hang on. You forgot my thirteenth birthday.'

'Never,' Llewellyn said fiercely. 'I sent a card every year. Even after you stopped sending them. Every birthday and every Christmas, until you were twenty-one. And then, I admit—yes, *then* I gave up.'

Rhys was still having trouble adjusting to the idea that his father hadn't ignored his birthdays after all. Or Christmas. So did it mean that his mother had got rid of the cards without telling him? He couldn't believe she'd do something so underhand. Yet Llewellyn's tone told him that his father wasn't lying. He really had sent the cards, and as Rhys and his mother had never moved, there was no way Llewellyn could have sent them to the wrong address.

'I was thirteen,' Rhys said. 'I still had a lot of growing up to do. And I was stroppy with it. I thought, well, if you weren't going to bother, neither was I.' Well, if this was going to be a day of revelations, he thought, it was time to be completely honest and open. Get rid of all the misunderstandings—or maybe confirm them. Confront them and put them behind him. 'I thought you'd got your new family, so weren't interested in me any more.'

'That's not true,' Llewellyn said. 'Yes, I have the girls. But I always loved you, always wanted you.' He sighed. 'I tried to see you after your mam and I split up. But whenever I came to the house to pick you up or take you back, there was a fight with your mam and it ended in tears. In the end I thought it was better to stay away, so you didn't get upset.' He shook his head in seeming frustration. 'I can see now it was the wrong thing to do, but I hated to see you cry. I sent cards, and I know it wasn't nearly enough—but back then I didn't know what else to do.'

'We saw you graduate, though,' Dilys put in, returning with a tray with mugs of coffee and a plate of sliced and buttered *bara brith*, Welsh tea bread, and placing the tray on the table.

Rhys blinked. 'You were there? But…how?'

'Myfanwy in the village used to keep your father posted. She knew your mam wasn't going, so she told us. We rang the university to find out where and what time and if we could get a ticket,' Dilys explained.

'I didn't see you there.'

'I didn't know if we'd be welcome,' Llewellyn said, 'so we kept out of the way. But I saw you up there on the stage and I was so proud of you. My son, the doctor.'

'You never said.'

'And *you* never asked,' Llewellyn countered.

Dilys cuffed her husband's arm. 'Don't be

awkward, Llewellyn. He's here now, and that's what matters.' She smiled at Rhys. 'We brought the girls up knowing they had a big brother and hoping that they'd meet him some day. If it was up to them, they'd have been here this afternoon, and they've already sent about fifty text messages to my phone between them saying, "Is he here yet?"' She placed a hand in front of her heart. 'Now, there's me running on, and I promised myself I wouldn't put pressure on you. It's just that we've waited so long and wanted so much...' Her eyes filled with tears. 'I'm so sorry, Rhys.'

'It's not your fault.' Rhys swallowed. 'And, just so you know, Dilys, I never blamed you for Dad leaving. I know he left well before he met you.'

'It was hard, with your mam.' Llewellyn grimaced. 'I lost my job when the pit closed. I couldn't provide for my family, so I didn't feel like a real man and I was hard to live with, too. And then...' He stopped.

Rhys knew exactly what his father couldn't say. So he was going to have to be the one to raise it. 'And then Gwyneth died.'

Llewellyn closed his eyes for a moment. 'I felt

so helpless. And it got worse and worse. In the end, I had to leave.' He sighed. 'I wanted to take you with me—but you were all your mam had. I couldn't be cruel enough to take you away from her.' He shook his head and rested a hand on his son's shoulder. 'We've lost years. But maybe now we can make a fresh start. Get to know each other—and in time you might come to see me as your father, not a distant stranger.'

'I'd like that,' Rhys said.

'And although I'm not your mam,' Dilys said, 'I've always thought of you in my head as one of mine.'

Rhys was too choked to answer in words. He simply hugged them both.

'Thank you, *cariad*,' Llewellyn said to Katrina. 'Thank you for bringing my boy back to me.'

The rest of the afternoon was a blur, with Dilys showing Rhys pictures of his half-sisters, Llewellyn showing them an old photograph of four-year-old Rhys holding baby Gwyneth and promising to get it copied for them, and Rhys and Katrina telling them both about the hospital and their life in London.

Rhys refused their invitation to stay for dinner.

'Not because I don't want to, but we're going back to London tonight—we're both on duty tomorrow. But I'll call you. And we'll see each other soon. Maybe you can come to London.'

'We'd like that, wouldn't we, Dilys?' Llewellyn said.

'Yes, and the girls will want to see you.' Dilys insisted on taking a photograph of him before they left, and Katrina took one of the three of them together on Dilys's camera as well as the camera on Rhys's mobile phone and her own.

'You have a safe journey, now,' Dilys told them, hugging them both goodbye. 'And we'll see you soon.'

When they drove away, Katrina was quiet.

'What are you thinking?' Rhys asked.

'If you'd grown up with Dilys and Llewellyn, you'd have had a very different life. You'd have been loved, Rhys, and you'd have *known* that you were loved.'

He shrugged. 'But maybe then I wouldn't have come to London. And I wouldn't have met you. And aren't you the one who always looks at the glass as half-full, not half-empty?'

'True.'

His mouth tightened briefly. 'I can't believe my mother actually kept my father's birthday and Christmas cards from me. I mean, what did she gain from it?'

'Maybe she was scared of losing you,' Katrina said. 'Maybe it was her way of holding on to you. If you thought she was your only family…'

'Hmm.' He sighed. 'Part of me wants to drop in and see her. Confront her. But that's not going to achieve a thing, just drive her even further away. I'm not sure you'll ever get the same kind of welcome from her as you did from Dilys.'

'It's OK.' Katrina reached across to cover his hand briefly on the steering wheel. 'Give it some time. No pressure.'

'Yes. Let's go home,' he said.

CHAPTER THIRTEEN

A FEW nights later, the phone shrilled, waking Rhys; he grabbed it and answered it without thinking. 'Rhys Morgan.'

'Now, that wasn't what I expected to hear.' Madison laughed.

Oh, lord. He'd answered Katrina's phone as if it were his own. And if her cousin hadn't known before that they were sleeping together, she definitely did now. 'I, um…'

'Relax. I'm teasing you. Good morning, Rhys.'

'Morning?' He glanced at the clock. Technically, it was morning. One o'clock in the morning. And then reality kicked in. Madison was thirty-seven weeks pregnant, according to Katrina. If she was calling at this time of the morning… 'Is everything all right?' he asked urgently.

'Yes. It's very all right.'

His heartbeat slowed back to normal. 'Good. But you need Katrina,' he guessed. He was pretty sure that Theo rather than Katrina would be Madison's birth partner, but they hadn't actually discussed it...so maybe Madison was in the early stages of labour and just wanted a bit of moral support from her cousin and best friend. He knew without having to be told that if either of them called for help at any time of day or night, the other would be straight there. 'Hang on.' He switched on the bedside light so Katrina could see his face, and handed the phone to her. 'It's Maddie, and she says everything's all right.'

'But?' Katrina's eyes widened with fear as she took the phone. 'Maddie? What aren't you telling me? What? Why didn't you tell me? Well, yes, of course he'd be panicking. Is...?'

Rhys gave up trying to follow the conversation. But the second Katrina ended the call, he looked straight at her. 'What's happened?'

'I'm an auntie.' She beamed at him. 'I'm an *auntie*!'

'Congratulations,' he said solemnly. 'Mother and baby both well?'

'Yes. Helen had a brilliant Apgar score, after an eight-hour labour—well, it was actually a bit longer than that because Maddie was being dopey and spent the whole day thinking she was having Braxton-Hicks' instead of the real thing. Seven pounds, Theo says she's the most beautiful baby he's ever seen, and…' She beamed again. 'I'd love to go and see her now, except the midwives would have my guts for garters. Maddie and Helen need some rest. But I'm going in before my shift tomorrow.' She paused. 'Um…you can say no, but if you want to come too, you'd be very welcome.'

He could see in her face that she really wanted him there.

And, surprisingly, he found that he wanted to be there too. Sharing the moment with Katrina—the first time she held the baby she'd so been looking forward to. 'I'd love to be there,' he said, meaning it.

The following morning, Rhys and Katrina were in the maternity ward at the crack of dawn.

'Congratulations, Maddie.' Katrina kissed her cousin, then hugged Theo. 'You, too, Theo. The florist isn't open yet, so you'll have to wait for the flowers.' She grinned. 'But I'm glad I'm first with a card.'

Theo coughed. 'Second. I was first.'

Rhys smiled. 'Second's fine by us. Congratulations, both of you. We brought you chocolates. And champagne.'

'And something I bought the day you got your amnio results.' Katrina handed Theo a beautifully wrapped parcel, then peered into the cot. 'Oh, she's gorgeous. And fast asleep.'

Rhys could hear the regret in her voice; Katrina was clearly dying to cuddle her new niece.

Obviously Madison could hear it, too. 'Asleep or awake, she needs her first cuddle from her Aunty Kat right this second.'

Katrina needed no second urging. She picked up her niece, sat on the edge of Madison's bed, and smiled.

Rhys had brought his camera, but he found himself unable to focus for a second. Because the sight of Katrina, with a newborn baby in her arms, made him realise what he really, really wanted out of life.

To be a family with Katrina.

To have children with her. He wanted to hear her telling stories to a little girl with blue eyes and a smile that made the room light up. He wanted to see her making sandcastles with a little boy who had floppy dark hair and was secure in his parents' love, the way he'd never been but the way he knew their children would definitely be. He wanted to share the same special kind of smiles with her that Theo and Maddie gave each other when they looked at their newborn.

'Rhys?' she asked.

He swallowed the lump in his throat and took the photographs. Managed to smile and chat to Theo and Maddie. And when it was his turn to cuddle the baby, he was utterly lost.

'You men are such frauds. There you are, doing the big, tough macho stuff, but give you a baby to hold and you're utter mush,' Madison accused, laughing.

Katrina joined in the laughter, but Rhys caught just a tiny shadow in her eyes.

Now wasn't the time and place to push her, but he'd ask her later. Make her talk to him, the way she'd made him talk to her. And whatever it was, he'd fix it for her, the way she'd helped to fix his own life.

Then Helen woke up, realised she was hungry and yelled.

'She needs her mummy,' Rhys said, and handed her back to Madison.

'And we have ward rounds and clinic,' Katrina said. 'But we'll be back later.' She stroked her niece's cheek, kissed Madison and Theo, and walked with Rhys to their own ward.

'You OK?' Rhys asked.

'Sure.' Katrina gave him a wide, bright smile.

Maybe he'd imagined it.

He put it to the back of his mind during ward rounds and his morning clinic. A bit of negotiation bought him an extended lunch break; he made an excuse to Katrina that he was due in clinic and didn't have time to go to see Maddie and the baby again, and instead went shopping.

For something very, very special.

At the end of his shift, he went to find Katrina.

She blinked. 'You're leaving early tonight?'

'Hey. I've made a real effort not to be quite such a workaholic,' he said.

She snorted. 'You mean you worked through your lunch-break.'

He didn't disabuse her of the idea but shepherded her to the staffroom. 'Come on. Time to go.'

'We're walking the wrong way,' Katrina said as he led her through the hospital gardens.

'So we are.' And the sun had set half an hour ago. He didn't care. Because he wanted the rest of his life to start right now. He threaded his fingers through hers. 'Humour me.'

She frowned. 'Rhys?'

He found a quiet bench and sat down, tugging her hand so that she joined him. 'I wanted to talk to you about something.'

'What?'

'Don't look so worried, *cariad*.' He smiled at her. 'This isn't brilliant timing, and it's not quite where I had in mind, but I can't wait any longer.'

She looked completely confused. 'Rhys?'

'I love you,' he said. 'And these last few months…I've come a long, long way. I always thought that I'd spend the rest of my life alone, because it's easier—because I didn't believe in family or marriage. But as I've got to know you, I've realised how wrong I was. The way I feel about you is deeper than I ever believed I could feel about anyone, and from seeing the way you are with your family I've discovered what a family really means. What marriage really means.'

He shifted so that he was on one knee. 'I want to be a family with you. So I'm asking you, Katrina Gregory—will you do me the honour of being my wife?'

'You want me to marry you?' she asked, looking slightly bewildered and as if she didn't quite believe that she'd heard him properly.

'I do,' he confirmed. 'Because I love you, Katrina. Heart and mind and body and soul. What you once told me about teamwork is so true—no matter what life throws at us, we'll get through it because we make a great team. My parents weren't lucky enough to have that together, but I can see now that my father has that kind of bond with Dilys. Your parents have it. Theo and Maddie have it. And I think we have it, too. I want to be with you for the rest of my life. Will you marry me?'

'Oh, Rhys.' She dropped to her knees and hugged him. 'Yes. *Yes*.'

Her kiss was as soft and sweet as she was. And all the empty spaces inside him were filled at last.

Eventually, he stood up and drew her to her feet. 'You've made me the happiest man alive, *cariad*. And I'll be a good husband to you, I swear.' He kissed her again. 'And father.'

'Father?'

He nodded. 'Seeing you cuddling little Helen this morning…it made me realise that was everything I want. You, and our children. If we're lucky enough.'

'Children.'

The flatness of her tone worried him. He knew she liked children—if she didn't, she'd hardly be working as a children's doctor and she definitely wouldn't spend her off-duty time telling them stories—not to mention the wonder in her face that morning when she'd cuddled her newborn niece—so it couldn't be that. But then he remembered the shadows in her eyes, earlier that day, and what she'd told him in the hospital canteen. 'Is this something to do with what Pete said?'

'He had a point.' Her voice was still flat, and the sparkle had gone from her eyes.

'No, he didn't. He didn't have a clue. You'll be a fantastic wife—just as I intend to be a fantastic husband to you. And you'll be brilliant mother.' The kind that his own mother hadn't been. Katrina was warm and loving, she listened—and she noticed.

She shook her head. 'Rhys, I sleep through thunderstorms. I'm bound to sleep through our baby crying in the night—and I'd never be able to forgive myself if I was needed and I didn't hear and our baby…' She dragged in a breath.

'Died?' He said the word she clearly couldn't bring herself to say.

She nodded.

He kissed her, very gently, then pulled back to make sure she could see his face. 'Katrina, that's not going to happen. I know you can't wear a hearing aid overnight, but that doesn't matter because I'm always going to be there. I'll hear.' He smiled. 'I might moan and groan a bit, and prod you and tell you it's your turn to get up and see to the baby, but I'll hear so you don't have to worry. And in the daytime we'll have one of those baby listeners with lights, the sort you can carry round with you and you can even turn the sound off but the flashing lights will tell you that the baby's crying. We'll work it out.' He stroked her hair. 'Remember what you said to me about teamwork? It goes both ways. I'm on your team, just as you're on mine. And if you're worrying about what Pete said, I can assure you that he was talking a load of rubbish.'

'Was he?'

She didn't sound so sure. 'Yes,' he said quietly. 'Because to me you're perfect, Katrina. You've shown me that anything is possible, with you by my side. You're warm and sweet and you're— oh, this sounds horribly corny, but I mean it— you're like sunshine. I love you just as you are. You'll be a fabulous mother, and we'll work perfectly as a team—we fill each other's gaps. You'll tell better stories than I will, and I'll hear crying more easily than you will. Simple.'

'Oh, Rhys.'

'It's all going to be fine. If you want children…'

She nodded. 'I do. Half the reason I'm so pleased that Maddie and Theo had Helen is because I never thought I'd have the chance to have children of my own—being an aunt to Maddie's baby is the next best thing.'

'I think,' he said, 'we need to work on this. Helen is definitely going to need a cousin—one who loves her just as much as you and Maddie love each other.'

Katrina's voice was slightly wobbly. 'Sounds good to me.'

'And now we've got that sorted…' He kissed her hand. 'I have to apologise to you. I misled you at lunchtime.'

She blinked. 'How?'

'I let you think I was working. I wasn't. But I did have something important to do.' He took the small box from his pocket. 'Something I wanted to give you.'

She opened it to find a narrow band of gold containing six stones.

'It's a cariad ring—the first letters of the names of the gemstones spell out the word "cariad". Which is Welsh for "dearest".' He smiled. 'Citrine, aquamarine, ruby, iolite—' a stone of such a deep blue that it was almost black '—amethyst and diamond. Though if you'd rather have a diamond solitaire then of course I'll buy you one.'

'No,' she said. 'I'd like a cariad ring. Because you call me that. And every time I see the ring I'll think of what you just said. *Cariad.*'

'It's what you are, Katrina. My heart's dearest.'

'Rhys, that's so romantic.' Tears shimmered in her eyes.

'Don't cry, *cariad*.' He brushed his mouth against hers. 'And it's Welsh gold.'

'But…don't you have to be royalty to buy Welsh gold?'

'No.' He grinned. 'Though, of course, to me you're a princess.'

She snorted. 'Wrong Gregory girl. Maddie does pink and girly.' Just like the tiny dress she'd given Maddie for her daughter, that morning. 'I don't.'

'I know. I was teasing you.' He brought her hand up to his mouth, kissed her ring finger and slid the ring on top of his kiss. 'This is a promise, Katrina. A promise that I'll always love you.'

'And you always keep your promises.' She reached up and kissed him. 'So do I. I'll always love you, Rhys.'

'Good.' His eyes held hers. 'So when are we getting married?'

'End of the summer?' she suggested.

He shook his head. 'Too far away. I love you, Katrina, and I don't want to have to wait for the rest of our lives together to start. Legally we could,' he said, 'get married in a fortnight.'

'We can't get married yet!' At his raised eyebrow, she explained, 'I want Maddie to be my bridesmaid. And she's only just had the baby.'

'True.' He thought for a moment. 'How about an Easter wedding? Though I want a compromise. As in a Valentine's Day dinner with our whole family—yours and mine—to celebrate our engagement.'

'Yes to the dinner—but there's no way we can get married at Easter. Even assuming everywhere isn't already booked solid, we don't have enough time to organise a wedding.'

'Sure we do.' He smiled. 'You leave it to me— all you need to do is the dresses. I assume you'd like a church wedding?'

'I think,' she said, 'as this is the only time I plan to get married, then yes—I can't deprive my dad of giving me away.'

'That's fine by me. So we need to see your parents. And talk to the vicar. And brief your bridesmaid. Ring your parents,' he said, 'and if they're free this evening I'll drive us to Suffolk.'

'Tonight?' she squeaked.

He shrugged. 'It'll take us, what, a couple of hours? That's doable.'

'But it's rush-hour, Rhys.'

'Doesn't matter. Anything's possible, with you by my side.'

'You're mad,' she said, smiling, 'but I love you.'

'Good.' He stole a kiss. 'Call your parents.'

Her parents were in, and Rhys was as good as his word. They were lucky with the traffic and two hours later they were sitting in her parents' house in Suffolk, and the Gregorys were hugging both Katrina and Rhys. Danny insisted on opening the champagne Rhys had brought, and Babs was delighted when Rhys asked if they could get married in the church in the village.

'Katrina was christened there.' She beamed. 'And you want to get married at Easter?'

'I don't want to wait any longer to start the rest of my life with Katrina,' Rhys said simply.

'There's an awful lot to organise in a very short space of time,' Danny said. 'But I can sort out a car for you, if you like.'

'Dad, I'll never be able to get in one of *your* cars, not with a wedding dress,' Katrina protested.

'Not one of mine,' he said. 'A friend of mine owns a white vintage Rolls Royce.'

'And I have a friend who makes wonderful cakes,' Babs said. 'You know Nicky, Kat.'

'Nicky who makes the best chocolate cake in the world?' Katrina checked. At her mother's nod, she smiled. 'Yes, please.'

Rhys laughed. 'Trust you to want a chocolate cake, *cariad*.'

'And we really need to talk to the vicar.' Danny glanced at his watch. 'Do you want me to call and see if we can pop in and see him now?'

'That,' Rhys said, 'would be brilliant. Thank you.'

'Anything we can do to help, just say the word,' Babs said. 'I promise you we won't be interfering in-laws. But as from now you're officially one of the Gregory family, and we look after our own.'

To Katrina's surprise, Rhys simply gave her mother a hug. 'Thank you. I can't think of any family I'd rather be part of.'

Katrina felt her eyes prickle. As Rhys had told her earlier, he'd come a long, long way. And wherever they went from here, he'd be right by her side.

CHAPTER FOURTEEN

'YOU'RE getting married?' Madison stared at Katrina in shock the next day when her cousin dropped in to see how her first day at home with the baby had gone. 'Hang on. When did all this happen?'

'Yesterday,' Katrina admitted.

'And you're engaged?'

'Rhys wants an official family dinner on Valentine's Day—which means you, Theo, Helen, Aunty Rose and Uncle Bryan as well—but, yes.' Katrina waggled her fingers to make the diamond in her engagement ring sparkle. 'This is a cariad ring.' She explained the significance of the gems to her cousin.

'That's *so* romantic, Kat.' Madison sighed. 'He's lovely. I *knew* he was going to be right for you. So have you set a date?'

'Easter.'

'What, this Easter?' At Katrina's nod, Madison shrieked, 'But that's only a couple of months away. No way can you organise a wedding that quickly! Or is it a register office do?'

'No, it's at St Mary's.'

'Our St Mary's, as in where we were both christened?'

'Yes.'

Madison blew out a breath. 'Cake. Reception. Dresses. Car. Flowers.' She ticked them off on her fingers and shook her head. 'No, you can't do it, Kat. I mean, I'll help as much as I can, but…it's just not doable.'

'You forget, I have two secret weapons. My mother and my fiancé.' Katrina spread her hands. 'Between them, Mum and Rhys already have all the bases covered. She's making the stationery— you know she loves doing that sort of thing— and your mum's doing the flowers. Nicky's making us a white chocolate wedding cake. Dad's sorting the car and Uncle Bryan's going to drive it, Rhys is talking to the King's Arms today and persuading them to do us a marquee and food and a band, and he says all I have to do is sort the dresses.' She smiled. 'Which is where you come in. And thank you, your offer of help is accepted.'

'Um, honey, Helen's three days old today. I don't think she's quite up to a trip to the shops just yet.'

'We're not going *shopping* shopping. We're going to do it online,' Katrina told her. 'No crowds, no hassle.' Exactly how she preferred to do her shopping.

'But you have to see the fabric to know if you like it.'

'No, I don't.'

'And shoes.'

'I *hate* shoe shopping, as you very well know.'

'Oh, you are so impossible, Katrina Gregory. I should set our mums on you.'

Katrina laughed. 'You can't. They're already involved in the plans. So are you going to help me choose our dresses, or what?'

'*Our* dresses?' Madison blinked.

'Well, who else would I ask to be my bridesmaid?'

Madison bit her lip. 'Kat, I've still got a baby belly. I'm not going to lose it by Easter.'

'You don't have to.' Katrina hugged her cousin. 'We'll find you something glam that looks fabulous. And you know you'd look gorgeous in a bin bag. You got the style gene in the family.'

'Hey, you're going to look fantastic as a bride.' Madison's eyes glittered wickedly. 'In a dress. You're actually going to buy a dress.'

'Don't rub it in.'

Madison grinned. 'Excellent. And I get to have a pink dress.'

Katrina groaned. 'No.'

'Raspberry?'

'No. That's pink.'

'Pale mulberry?'

'That's pink, too.'

'You're so bossy,' Madison grumbled.

'Because you taught me how,' Katrina retorted.

Two hours later, they'd found the perfect outfits. And shoes to match. And everything was going to be delivered to Madison's house to make sure that Rhys didn't actually see the wedding dress beforehand.

Everyone on the ward was just as pleased for Katrina and Rhys as their families had been, and Katrina was surprised by just how quickly every-

thing fell into place between her mother's orga-
nising skills and Rhys's.

'One thing,' Rhys said. 'I need to find a best
man.'

'How about your best friend from your student
days? Someone in Cardiff? Or someone on the
ward—maybe Will?' she suggested. 'And I'm
sure he'd make an exception and wear a sensible
tie for the day.'

'Actually, I was thinking—if you don't mind—
of asking my father,' Rhys said hesitantly. 'I
mean, it's still early days…but it's kind of a
show of faith. To show that in future our relationship will be what it should be.'

'That,' Katrina said softly, 'would be perfect.'
Though there was one sticking point—one that
had to be voiced. 'Would your mother mind?'

'She's probably not even going to turn up—to
the wedding or to our engagement dinner.' He
sighed. 'I'm sorry, Katrina. I can't give you in-
laws as nice as the ones you're giving me.'

'Yes, you can. There's Llewellyn and Dilys.
And I'm looking forward to meeting the girls
this weekend.'

'Me, too.' He held her close. 'Right now, life's

better than I ever imagined it could possibly be, even in my wildest dreams.'

'And it's going to stay this good,' she promised him.

Rhiannon, Sian and Mair turned out to be just like their mother: warm and open and talkative. Katrina liked them immediately—and they all adored Rhys.

'There was a reason why I asked you to London,' Rhys said. 'Apart from to see you, that is.' He took four envelopes from his jacket pocket and handed one to Llewellyn and Dilys, and one each to his half-sisters.

'We're to open them now?' Rhiannon asked.

'Now,' Rhys said with a smile.

Dilys opened the envelope and scanned the invitation quickly. 'You're getting married at Easter?' Dilys stared at them in surprise, and then beamed. 'That's fabulous. And you're sure you want us to come?'

'Absolutely,' Katrina said. 'It's not going to be an enormous wedding, as my family's quite small—just our family and closest friends—but there'll be more of a party in the evening when our colleagues will be there too.'

'We'd love to come,' Dilys said immediately. 'All of us.'

'There was something else.' Rhys coughed, and turned to Llewellyn. 'I was wondering if you'd be my best man.'

'Your best man?' Llewellyn echoed, looking shocked. 'I...I'd be proud. Really proud and really honoured.' His eyes were bright with unshed tears. 'As long as it won't upset your mam,' he added, looking awkward.

Rhys gave a half-shrug. 'She probably won't be there.'

Llewellyn sighed. 'She's not softened at all over the years, then?'

'You know the situation,' Rhys said. 'But at least you're all going to be there, so my family's going to be part of my wedding day.'

'We wouldn't miss it,' Dilys said warmly, 'not for anything.'

'And one more thing,' Katrina said. 'We'd like to have an official engagement dinner. Just our families. On Valentine's Day.'

The day of the engagement dinner arrived swiftly. The Gregorys and the Morgans took to each other straight away, and Katrina was delighted by the way Rhys seemed to bloom in their company.

But during the dinner Rhys took her hand, nodding at the family sitting a few tables down from them.

She looked, and saw the same thing that he did: a small boy coughing and apparently finding it hard to breathe.

'I think one of us might be needed there, *cariad*,' he said quietly. 'Could be a foreign body, could be asthma. I'll go.'

She watched him walk over to the family and talk to the parents—and then he beckoned her over.

'Kat, it's your engagement. Stay here. I'll go and help Rhys,' Theo offered.

Madison placed her hand over his. 'Let her go,' she said softly. 'They're used to working together.'

'Like we are,' Theo said. 'Point taken.'

'I won't be long,' Katrina said, and went to join Rhys.

Rhys introduced her swiftly, and continued taking the patient history. Katrina noticed that the little boy was wheezing heavily, though in a way that was a good sign. The last thing she wanted to see was a 'silent chest', where very little air was going in and out of the child's lungs and breathing sounds were completely absent— a silent chest was life-threatening, and the child would need high-flow oxygen therapy and steroid injections as emergency treatment.

'Ben's been wheezing a bit today—we shouldn't have taken him for such a long walk in the cold, but we were having such a nice time we didn't think about the temperature,' the woman said, biting her lip.

Definitely asthma, then, and this attack had been brought on by the cold. 'Has he had asthma long?' Katrina asked.

'Since he was about three. The doctor diagnosed him three years ago.'

'Do you have his reliever inhaler?' Rhys asked.

Even as he spoke, the woman was rummaging through her bag. 'Oh, no. It must still be in our room.'

'Can you get it, please?' Rhys asked. 'And do you have a spacer?'

'A spacer?' she asked.

Clearly not. 'Never mind—I can make something. But we need his medication right now, please.'

A waitress came over to them. 'Can I help?'

Katrina nodded. 'Please. Do you have a polystyrene cup and a knife? Or any cup where we can cut a hole in.'

'If necessary, a brown paper bag,' Rhys added. 'And call an ambulance.'

'Ambulance?' The little boy's father went white.

'Precautionary,' Rhys said gently. 'The medications and a makeshift spacer might be enough to get him through this, but I don't have a medical kit with me and we never, ever take risks with little ones.'

Meanwhile Katrina picked the little boy up, sat on his chair and settled him on her lap. Laying him down would make things a lot worse, she knew; right now he needed to be upright, to help him breathe. And being unable to breathe properly was making him panic, which in turn made it even harder for him to breathe—a vicious circle she needed to break by distracting him.

'My name's Katrina,' she said, 'and, although I don't look like one right now, I'm a doctor, just like Rhys. I'm going to help you feel better, sweetheart. Is that OK?'

He nodded, clearly not having the breath or the energy to speak. Not a good sign, she thought.

'Now, I'm going to undo the button on your collar to make you feel a bit more comfortable, and then I'm going to tell you a story. Do you like pirates?'

He nodded, and she quickly undid the button, checked his pulse and counted his breathing rate, and palpated his neck muscles to check whether he was using them to help him breathe—which would mean he was really struggling.

'Rhys, his resps are forty and his pulse is one-thirty,' she said quietly. 'Using neck muscles.'

He nodded and she knew he'd got the message. Ben was having a severe asthma attack; his heart rate and breathing rate were both faster than they should be, as she'd expected, but she'd be more worried if his heart rate suddenly dropped.

She began telling a story to Ben while she kept an eye on his respiration and pulse.

'So how often does Ben take the preventer inhaler, the brown one?' Rhys asked Ben's father.

'I don't know. Three or four times a week.'

'And does he have many attacks like this?' Rhys asked.

'Not really—once every few months, but not as bad as this. We try to keep him away from cats and pollen, because we know they set his asthma off.'

'Any other triggers?'

Ben's father shook his head. 'Not that we know of.'

'OK.' Rhys touched Katrina's hand and mouthed, 'Pulse and resps?'

'Still one-thirty and forty,' she mouthed back.

But at least her story was keeping the little boy calm, Rhys thought with relief.

The waitress came back with a polystyrene cup and a knife. 'Is this all right, Dr Morgan?'

'It's perfect. Thank you,' Rhys said.

'And the ambulance is on its way. It should be here in fifteen minutes.'

'That's great. Thanks.' Rhys smiled at her. 'Now, what I'm going to do is make a hole in the bottom of this,' he explained to Ben's father. 'It'll make the medication more effective because he'll get more medicine into his lungs than he would if he just takes the inhaler on its own.'

A moment later, Ben's mother hurried across the room to him with the inhaler. Swiftly, Rhys made a hole in the end of the polystyrene cup that was just enough to fit the opening of the inhaler, shook the inhaler and fitted it in place. 'Ben, *bach*, I'm going to put the end of the cup over your face and I'm going to ask you to breathe while I count. Can you do that for me?' he asked.

The little boy nodded.

Rhys gave him one puff of the medication. 'That's great, Ben. Slow, deep breath in—that's it—and out.' He counted four more slow breaths for the little boy.

'Shouldn't you give him more, to get it into him more quickly?' Ben's father asked anxiously.

'No, if you do more than one at a time the droplets of the spray stick together and coat the sides of the spacer, so Ben would get less medicine, not more,' Katrina explained.

Rhys removed the inhaler, shook it again, fitted it back into the makeshift spacer and repeated the dose of medication.

'Has he been in hospital before with his asthma?' Katrina asked.

'No,' Ben's mother replied.

'So this must be pretty scary for you. They'll put him on oxygen in the ambulance, and they'll put a little cap on his finger so they can measure the amount of oxygen in his blood—it won't hurt him at all, but if you've not seen it before it's worrying to see your child attached to monitors,' she said. 'They might need to give him some additional medication, depending on how quickly he responds to this—and they'll give you an asthma review. If he's using a reliever inhaler three times a week, as you said, his asthma isn't properly controlled, and they'll need to think about giving Ben something different for a preventer inhaler.'

While Katrina talked, she was checking Ben's pulse. It was still too fast.

'So you see this thing a lot?' Ben's father asked.

Katrina nodded. 'We both work on the children's ward. We've seen little ones much worse than this pull round, so try not to worry.'

Rhys was still administering medication,

though, as Ben wasn't yet responding, Katrina was very glad he'd called an ambulance.

'Are you staying here,' she asked, 'or are you local?'

'On holiday—it's half-term,' Ben's mother explained.

'It's a nice part of the world. And you have to take him to Walberswick—it's really pretty on the coast,' Katrina said with a smile.

'So you're local?'

'Local-born,' Katrina said. 'We're just staying here for a couple of days.'

'And we've spoiled your holiday.' Ben's father bit his lip. 'I'm so sorry.'

'We're not exactly on holiday,' Rhys said as he shook the inhaler again. 'We're celebrating our engagement.'

'Your engagement? Congratulations. Oh, and this is the last thing you need, the night of your—' Ben's mother began.

'We're doctors. This is what we do,' Rhys cut in gently. 'We couldn't sit by and see Ben struggle like this. Not when we can help.'

'Absolutely,' Katrina confirmed, stroking Ben's hair. To her relief, she felt the wheezing start to ease. Rhys looked at her, got the message she mouthed to him, and the worry left his eyes.

By the time the ambulance arrived, Ben was breathing much more normally. 'He still needs to go in, though, to be checked over,' Rhys warned, and he and Katrina went to the ambulance door with the paramedics to give them Ben's medical history and explain what they'd done.

When they walked back into the restaurant, people at the other tables stood up and clapped.

'It's our job. We didn't do anything special,' Rhys said.

'Yes, you did.' Mair, the youngest of Llewellyn and Dilys's girls, came over to him and hugged him. 'My brother, the hero. I'm *so* proud of you.'

Rhys hugged her back, not saying anything, but Katrina could see in his eyes that finally he felt part of his family, that he was accepted and valued exactly for who he was—and she could feel tears pricking her own eyelids.

'I'm afraid we had to send your puddings back,' Babs said. 'Your ice cream melted and Rhys's apple crumble went cold, but I'll ask the waitress to bring you a replacement.'

Katrina smiled. 'Thanks, Mum. I don't want a pudding now, though. I'm fine.'

'Same here,' Rhys agreed. 'Too full of adrenalin.'

'I wouldn't say no to coffee, though,' Katrina said. 'Especially as I know what the petits fours are like here.'

Danny laughed. 'I'll go and sort it out. Coffees all round, yes?'

When he'd gone, Sian asked, 'So that's the sort of thing you both do all day? Saving lives like that?'

'Not all day,' Rhys explained. 'It's usually the emergency department who'd deal with a severe asthma attack and then once the patient's stable they'd send him or her up to us. But we do have an emergency assessment clinic and the doctors take turns running it.'

'We have other clinics, too. Plus we have ward rounds twice a day to check up on the children we're looking after who are staying in,' Katrina added.

'And my wife-to-be here spends half an hour a day in the playroom on the ward, after her shift, telling stories.' Rhys slid his arm round her shoulders. 'I told her off the first day we worked together. Told her she was getting too involved with her patients. And I'm very pleased to say I've learned that she's absolutely right.'

Shortly after Danny returned to the table, the waitress brought them coffee.

Dilys nudged Llewellyn. 'Now would be a good time.'

'Good time for what?' Rhys asked.

'To give you both this.' Llewellyn took a parcel from under the table and handed it to Katrina. 'It's traditional.'

Katrina undid the ribbon, opened the box and unwrapped the tissue paper to reveal a carved wooden spoon.

'It's a Welsh love spoon,' Rhys said.

'Symbolic,' Llewellyn said. 'With a heart, horseshoe and a celtic knot—it means love, good luck, and everlasting.'

'It's beautiful,' Katrina said.

Dilys nudged her husband again. 'Tell her the rest of it.'

Llewellyn flushed, but said nothing.

'Men,' Dilys said, rolling her eyes. 'He carved it for you himself. He's been working on it ever since we got back from London, after you gave us the wedding invitation.'

'I just wanted it to be special,' Llewellyn said simply.

'It is.' Rhys's voice was slightly cracked.

This was a gift straight from the heart, Katrina knew. 'We'll treasure it always. Thank you.'

CHAPTER FIFTEEN

AFTER that, time seemed to race by, and then it was the day of the wedding. 'We're not going to need confetti,' Madison said, walking into Katrina's bedroom. 'It's snowing.'

'It can't be. It's Easter,' Katrina said.

'And Easter's early this year. Take a look out of the window.'

Katrina did so. Huge flakes of slow were drifting down and settling lightly on the ground.

'Your wedding pictures are going to be absolutely stunning,' Madison told her.

True, but something else was worrying her more. 'What about Helen? She's only two months old.'

'Stop fussing. She's having a wonderful time, being cuddled by her dad and having her grandmother and her great-uncle cooing over her. Besides, you and I have some seriously girly stuff to do. Even if you were too mean to let me have a pink dress.' She smiled at Katrina and tugged at the towel Katrina had wrapped turban-style round her wet hair. 'Starting with this.'

'I need to do something first.' Katrina grabbed her mobile phone and sent a text to Rhys. *I love you. See you in church.*

He must have been waiting for her text, she thought, because he replied immediately. *Love you too. And I can't wait to carry you over the threshold tonight.*

Madison groaned. 'That text was obviously from Rhys. I know brides are supposed to be blushing, but it's going to play havoc with your make-up if you do that now. Think of…I dunno. Stop thinking about whatever your husband-to-be just suggested and start mentally naming all the bones in the body, or something.'

'I'm getting married,' Katrina said. 'To Rhys. Today. I'm really getting married.'

Madison hugged her. 'And you look absolutely radiant. I'm thrilled for you, I really am. But if we don't start getting you ready, hon, we're going to be late.'

Katrina wrinkled her nose. 'Let's skip the

make-up, then. Because I promised him I wouldn't be late.'

'You are *not* skipping the make-up on your wedding day,' Madison informed her. 'I'll just be quicker about it than I would have been. Now, sit still while I do your hair. Mum says the flowers at the church are all done, your bouquet's here, the buttonholes for our lot are downstairs and Dad—if we can prise him away from his granddaughter—is going to drop the ones for Rhys's family at the hotel.' She paused. 'So is Rhys's mum going to turn up?'

'I have no idea,' Katrina said. 'I hope so, for his sake.'

'On the other hand,' Madison said dryly, 'if she's going to be a nightmare and make everyone miserable, it might be better if she stays away.'

'Whichever way, he's going to be hurt.'

'Hey. He has you. And when you walk down the aisle to him today, he's going to be lit up from the inside. You make him happy, Kat. And he's the best thing that's ever happened to you, too.'

Half an hour later, Madison pronounced Katrina's hair, make-up and nails satisfactory. 'Don't put the dress on yet,' she warned. 'Right.

Final checklist before I start getting ready. Something old?'

'Mum's pearls.'

'Good, that's borrowed we can tick off as well. New's your dress. Blue? Oh, no, I meant to buy you a garter!' She slapped a hand to her forehead. 'I'm so sorry, honey. You picked a rubbish bridesmaid.'

'No, I picked the best. And you've had a brand-new baby to think about. That's far more important than a blue garter.' Katrina smiled. 'Besides, I bought some hold-up stockings. And the tops just happen to be blue lace.'

'Brilliant. I think,' Madison said, 'we're sorted. I'll go down and get us a cup of tea, and then I'll do my make-up and we'll get you into your dress when we've finished our tea.'

As if on cue, there was a rap at the door and Katrina's mother walked in. 'Tea.'

Madison beamed at her. 'Perfect timing. You're an angel. Thanks, Aunt Babs.'

'I don't think I've ever seen you looking so lovely,' Babs said to Katrina. 'I think I'm really going to need tissues in the church.'

'The mother of the bride is supposed to cry

buckets,' Madison said with a grin. 'Underneath her fabulous hat. And from what Mum tells me, your hat is astonishingly good.'

Babs laughed. 'That's because Rose came with me to help choose it.'

'So is there anything I need to do?' Katrina asked.

'Just look beautiful. Everything's under control. Bryan's taken the buttonholes over to the King's Arms, and he brought Rose back from the church—she did the honeysuckle this morning just in case it wilted overnight.'

The church was going to be decorated with winter flowering honeysuckle from Katrina's parents' garden—the same flower that was threaded through the bride's bouquet of ivory roses—and Rose had also suggested putting little vases of snowdrops and tealight candles in clear glass holders on the shelf on the back of each pew.

'The church is going to look absolutely stunning. The perfect wedding,' Madison said happily. 'Candlelight, snow, roses, and the feel you can only get from a wedding in an ancient country church.'

There was a knock at the door. 'Delivery for

the bride.' Katrina recognised the voice as Theo's.

'You can't come in, Kat's not dressed!' Madison called. 'Hang on. I'll come and fetch it.'

'That's just an excuse to give his wife-to-be a kiss,' Katrina teased. Madison and Theo had set a date for their own wedding for the first of May.

'Be quiet and drink your tea, you,' Madison retorted with a grin.

When Madison left the room, Babs hugged her daughter. 'You look so beautiful, darling. And I know how much Rhys loves you—he's put so much into making today perfect for you. This is going to be one of the happiest days of my life,' she said.

'Mine, too,' Katrina said softly. And she really, really hoped it would be like that for Rhys, too. That he wouldn't let his mother's bitterness spoil this for him.

'Delivery from the groom,' Madison said as she walked back in. 'He's sent you a sprig of myrtle, which he says has to go in your bouquet for luck and then be given to me afterwards, so Mum's sorting that. And he also sent this for you.'

It was a single deep red rose, with a card. Katrina recognised Rhys's spiky handwriting and opened it, then smiled.

'What does it say, then?' Madison demanded.

'I love you,' Katrina said simply.

Madison rolled her eyes. 'I love you, too. But… Oh. Duh. Of course he loves you. He's going to get married to you this morning.'

Katrina laughed. 'I love you too, Maddie. And I don't think I've ever been so…' She swallowed hard.

'No, no, no.' Madison crossed her hands rapidly. 'Don't cry, hon. You can't cry on your wedding day, even if they're happy tears.' She hugged her cousin. 'Drink your tea while I get my face on.'

'You've got half an hour before the car leaves,' Babs told them. 'And I, meanwhile, am going to steal my great-niece for a cuddle.'

Twenty-five minutes later, they were both ready. Katrina and Madison stood side by side in front of the cheval mirror, staring at their reflections.

'You look stunning,' Katrina said softly. Madison's dress was made from wine-coloured chiffon with a V-neck, a V-back and a gathered empire bodice that flattered her post-baby figure and also made her look taller. Her stole was in matching chiffon and, with Madison's dark hair worn loose, the outfit looked incredible.

'So do you,' Madison breathed. 'On me, that dress would look appalling. I'm too short and too round. But because you're tall and slender and gorgeous... It's just fantastic.' Katrina's ivory dress was bias cut, with a scoop neckline, ending in a puddle train. With her mother's pearls at choker length round her neck and a simple pearl tiara and a short pearl-edged veil, she looked the perfect bride. 'I'm so proud of you,' Madison said. 'My little better-than-sister.'

'Don't cry. You'll set me off again,' Katrina warned huskily.

There was a rap at the door. 'Are you ready yet? The car's going to have to leave,' Babs called.

'Come in, Mum.'

Babs walked in and swallowed hard. 'Look at you both. I...' She shook her head. 'Our girls, Rose. They look amazing.'

'Our girls,' Rose echoed, coming in with the bouquets. 'Oh, my lord. There's not going to be a dry eye in the church. You both look fantastic.'

'Car,' Madison said. 'Now. Before you make her cry and ruin her make-up.' But she, too, was sniffing slightly.

Danny held his daughter's hand in the car all the way to the church, too overcome to say anything after he'd hugged her and told her how proud he was of her. Madison was waiting for them in the porch, peering out of the heavy oak doors to see where they'd got to.

'Message from the bridegroom,' she said. 'You have a last-minute wedding guest.'

Katrina blinked at her. 'Rhys's mum? She decided to come after all?'

Madison nodded and made last-minute adjustments to Katrina's veil. 'Don't worry. Rhys is fine. He's smiling. I think his mum's going to cry in a minute, but so is your mum and mine and Dilys—it's what mums are meant to do at weddings. Oh, and Rhys says to tell you he loves you.' She stood back for a moment. 'Oh, Kat. You look wonderful. You and Rhys are going to look so perfect together—because you *are* perfect together.' Swallowing back her tears, she moved into her position as bridesmaid.

And when Katrina walked down the aisle on her father's arm a few moments later, Pachelbel's 'Canon' playing softly, and she saw the joy and love in Rhys's face as he turned to look at her, she knew that her cousin was right. She and Rhys were perfect together—and everything was going to be just fine.

MEDICAL™

Large Print

Titles for the next six months...

October

A FAMILY FOR HIS TINY TWINS	Josie Metcalfe
ONE NIGHT WITH HER BOSS	Alison Roberts
TOP-NOTCH DOC, OUTBACK BRIDE	Melanie Milburne
A BABY FOR THE VILLAGE DOCTOR	Abigail Gordon
THE MIDWIFE AND THE SINGLE DAD	Gill Sanderson
THE PLAYBOY FIREFIGHTER'S PROPOSAL	Emily Forbes

November

THE SURGEON SHE'S BEEN WAITING FOR	Joanna Neil
THE BABY DOCTOR'S BRIDE	Jessica Matthews
THE MIDWIFE'S NEW-FOUND FAMILY	Fiona McArthur
THE EMERGENCY DOCTOR CLAIMS HIS WIFE	Margaret McDonagh
THE SURGEON'S SPECIAL DELIVERY	Fiona Lowe
A MOTHER FOR HIS TWINS	Lucy Clark

December

THE GREEK BILLIONAIRE'S LOVE-CHILD	Sarah Morgan
GREEK DOCTOR, CINDERELLA BRIDE	Amy Andrews
THE REBEL SURGEON'S PROPOSAL	Margaret McDonagh
TEMPORARY DOCTOR, SURPRISE FATHER	Lynne Marshall
DR VELASCOS' UNEXPECTED BABY	Dianne Drake
FALLING FOR HER MEDITERRANEAN BOSS	Anne Fraser

MILLS & BOON®

MEDICAL™

Large Print

January

THE VALTIERI MARRIAGE DEAL	Caroline Anderson
THE REBEL AND THE BABY DOCTOR	Joanna Neil
THE COUNTRY DOCTOR'S DAUGHTER	Gill Sanderson
SURGEON BOSS, BACHELOR DAD	Lucy Clark
THE GREEK DOCTOR'S PROPOSAL	Molly Evans
SINGLE FATHER: WIFE AND MOTHER WANTED	Sharon Archer

February

EMERGENCY: WIFE LOST AND FOUND	Carol Marinelli
A SPECIAL KIND OF FAMILY	Marion Lennox
HOT-SHOT SURGEON, CINDERELLA BRIDE	Alison Roberts
A SUMMER WEDDING AT WILLOWMERE	Abigail Gordon
MIRACLE: TWIN BABIES	Fiona Lowe
THE PLAYBOY DOCTOR CLAIMS HIS BRIDE	Janice Lynn

March

SECRET SHEIKH, SECRET BABY	Carol Marinelli
PREGNANT MIDWIFE: FATHER NEEDED	Fiona McArthur
HIS BABY BOMBSHELL	Jessica Matthews
FOUND: A MOTHER FOR HIS SON	Dianne Drake
THE PLAYBOY DOCTOR'S SURPRISE PROPOSAL	Anne Fraser
HIRED: GP AND WIFE	Judy Campbell

millsandboon.co.uk Community

Join Us!

The Community is the perfect place to meet and chat to kindred spirits who love books and reading as much as you do, but it's also the place to:

- **Get the inside scoop from authors about their latest books**
- **Learn how to write a romance book with advice from our editors**
- **Help us to continue publishing the best in women's fiction**
- **Share your thoughts on the books we publish**
- **Befriend other users**

Forums: Interact with each other as well as authors, editors and a whole host of other users worldwide.

Blogs: Every registered community member has their own blog to tell the world what they're up to and what's on their mind.

Book Challenge: We're aiming to read 5,000 books and have joined forces with The Reading Agency in our inaugural Book Challenge.

Profile Page: Showcase yourself and keep a record of your recent community activity.

Social Networking: We've added buttons at the end of every post to share via digg, Facebook, Google, Yahoo, technorati and de.licio.us.

www.millsandboon.co.uk

MILLS & BOON

www.millsandboon.co.uk

- ◎ All the latest titles
- ◎ Free online reads
- ◎ Irresistible special offers

And there's more...

- ◎ Missed a book? Buy from our huge discounted backlist
- ◎ Sign up to our FREE monthly eNewsletter
- ◎ eBooks available now
- ◎ More about your favourite authors
- ◎ Great competitions

Make sure you visit today!

www.millsandboon.co.uk